"Kate Tough is such a clever writer. Without question – massively recommended. I loved this collection."

— **DAISY HOLLANDS**

"Fantastic collection. On point for the digital and #metoo generation. A required read. This author never patronises."

— **SUE MAC**

"Had me cackling on my bed at night, scaring the cat laughing. I haven't found this much honesty in a book in a very long time."

— **MERCEDES DIAZ**

"Taut and unflinching. Should appeal to fans of TV series Fleabag."

— ***THE LADY MAGAZINE ON KEEP WALKING, RHONA BEECH***

"A brilliant observation on relationships and friendships. Along with tears and anger, there's laughter and hope."

— ***HELLO MAGAZINE ON KEEP WALKING, RHONA BEECH***

KISSING LYING DOWN

NINE STORIES

KATE TOUGH

PICÓN PRESS

First published in 2020 by PICÓN PRESS

Interior author photo by Ana Dominguez.

www.katetough.com

CONTENT WARNING: The closing paragraphs of the story 'Kissing Lying Down' contain sexual assault, and the closing paragraphs of 'And Maybe It Will Turn Out That Was Enough' depict suicide.

"In nuclear physics, an inelastic collision is one in which the incoming particle causes the nucleus it strikes to become excited or to break up."

Wikipedia

"And 'who' 'am' 'I'? Embracing you & failure's changed all that 'cause now I know I'm no one. And there's a lot to say..."

Chris Kraus, *I Love Dick*

CONTENTS

TIED UP WITH STRING

Another thing Sheridan has never got used to about Ross is his expressionless sex face. He's almost soundless too but that's par for the course: guys rarely make much noise except when a few beers have featured (*uh-UH-I'm gonna co-o-ome!*). The exception was the one who'd moaned and bucked like a porn actress when she'd touched his nipples, so she hadn't gone near them again. Cruel? Anyone who'd seen it would have done the same. Point being, other men had at least adjusted their facial muscles to signal commitment to the task.

Unlike Ross. Who last night had arrived home chipper about the holidays – twelve days off over Christmas and New Year – and he'd poured wine and sidled in on Sheridan when she was reheating soup, until she had to turn off the gas while he manhandled her cardigan. Losing patience and yanking it sent two ladybird buttons onto the tiles. Proceedings halted. "Can I help it if your clothes are from Tesco?" was his response, and she wasn't sure if it was in jest, given the deadpan delivery.

Increasingly she's found herself musing on the sex face of every passing man – an unsettling occupation given that it's the early hours of Christmas Eve, in a queue for a night bus. Except Sheridan isn't in the queue, she's hovering behind a pillar of the Dental Hospital because the mood on Sauchiehall Street might be jovial, but she's seen what it's like when the mood is off and it's six o'clock news stuff (once she'd had to walk by two bare-chested men hunting one another down the middle of the road, dragging and slamming each other onto the tarmac so cars were forced to crawl around them, while the nearest policemen had photos taken with a hen party). If she'd known Ross then he'd have been beside her muttering, "Stellar use of taxes."

Tonight's jostling frangible festivity reminds her of the dodgems at a funfair, where no one can quite trust the rule changes (Doof! Bang! *Ha ha!*). She watches as a guy standing in the Perspex shelter barely breaks his sentence to bend to one side and throw up. The foamy pool shines as he talks to the slumped girl in the undersized dress, slingbacks dangling from her thumb.

Why's Sheridan involved herself in this? To avoid a ninety minute cab wait and the post-midnight fare (it's Ross who can afford their three-bed house and taxis back). Sheridan misses the six quid journeys to the last flat she rented – the one walkable from here, except in the rain or high heels. What was it about her, she used to wonder, that turned taxi compartments into two halves of a confessional? As soon as a word was uttered by either party, *sploosh*, floodgates – is there a Glasgow taxi driver's life story she hasn't heard?

There was the one who used to be a car salesman in a target-driven hellhole where he was bawled at and humiliated for motivation and when he complained, it didn't exactly improve his situation (bless him for thinking it would). "But ah don't regret speakin up for myself, ah just regret how long it took me tae walk. S'night an day, workin for maself, wife's happier an all, might enrol in the open uni sometime, ah just never stuck in at school, though ma mother —" (Okay! Let's move this along!).

That much life story doesn't fit in a six quid taxi ride, no sir, she got *that* much life story when they kept her waiting outside her flat, engine idling, chapter after chapter, and she handed them a tip for the privilege. Her penance for going out on weeknights – they'd never have sat there like priest and confessor if the pavements had been weekend-teeming.

Though drunk or tired on her side of the glass, Sheridan held on to those drivers' pearls. She could handle losing scarves, a tenner here or there, but hated losing moments that only took place because of the people in them. That breed of carelessness would show her up as a shoddy custodian. Which she wasn't.

She hasn't mislaid Ross. Hasn't left him in a bar after an argument. Nope, he set off after breakfast to see his children near Stoke, in service to a spreadsheet apportioning 24—26th December into slots when the kids are either with their mother, or in a hotel with him ('tis the season to be jolly!). Sheridan went with him the first year of their relationship and his kids were so passive-aggressive with her that she offered not to go in future. Ross proffered no protest and the following year Sheridan conjured such a good way to spend Christmas that she's done it both years since: it's a four-day plan, starting with a girls' get-together on the 23rd then the late bus home.

When the double-decker approaches she joins the queue then asks the driver what the fare is. Fully preoccupied with imagining his sex face, she doesn't hear the answer and has to check again. His disdain is so similar to Ross's it saves her the bother of her game.

As the bus accelerates, the teen beside Sheridan is using her as a backrest which she doesn't take personally (or predatorily – he won't have registered her as relevant). Does she say anything? No. It's a packed deck. Does she want to say anything? Make yourself comfortable, what does she care, it's *Christmas*. He's slurring to his friend across the aisle and she makes the effort not to imagine their sex faces.

Her phone beeps. A friend asking, *Home safe*? Though when she checks it's Ross, saying, **Can't sleep. Wanna help?**

Been thinking about you, she replies, because it amuses her, adding, **I'm on the bus, can't...**

- **Keep your voice low, no one cares**

- **I care**

- **Quick photo between your legs?**

Sheridan aims her phone at the floor between her feet, clicks and sends the picture. No reply. Did he laugh?

Her very own Sir Lancelot, sexting requests from a Premier Inn in Stoke. His car boot filled with boxes which were smothered in shiny paper by Sheridan – most of her Sunday (a small price). She and Ross swapped gifts before he set off, unleashing the other face of his she can't get used to, which has to stem from his 'only child' experience – no one to tease him out of it. Imagine: schoolgirl finding a boy band at the breakfast table. Sheridan puts less and less effort into choosing presents, hoping for a normal face on opening. It never works, no matter how bad the gift: nasal grooming kit, wine thermometer, joke-shop apron with boobs (she hoped a vaguely kinky item might trigger the dead-kipper face rather than the musical-theatre lead). She resorted to brown paper this year to set a subdued tone, but Ross called it 'vintage' and squeaked as he tore at it.

A far cry from her years with Nate, who hadn't cared a whit. After they'd realised they were only exchanging parcels in case the other would be offended, they were able to stop. So when she's shopping for Ross, she doesn't have to feel guilty about putting more effort into buying something for Nate. She'll simply turn up tomorrow after a two-hour drive. That's her present to him. And he'll open the door and have a meal waiting. His present to her.

She's sitting too near a millennial's phone conversation to tune it out.

"She took their menus away and they hadn't ordered yet!"

"*I know*, I nearly said to her, 'Are you on drugs or something?'"

"I just said to him, 'That's disgusting language and you need to leave.'"

"He asked if the rug matched the curtains."

"*Rug* – doesn't matter. Hello?"

"I've zero notes to get my family anything." Long pause.

"Punch yourself in the arm right now or you'll end up more depressed."

Longer pause.

"Fuck *off*! Where? At *karaoke*? What's he *like*?"

Oh how Sheridan lives for the pauses. And oh how she wants to grab the handset: *I'm giddy you've met someone. And if he can sing? Fantastic. And if he grunts during sex with a smile on his face? Woo, lottery win! But unless he's a real, solid good 'un, RUN. All I can tell you in my most serious voice, is that the easiest time to end a relationship is at the start.*

It's no newsflash that Sheridan thinks about ending things with Ross, for instance, so they don't become that couple they see on holiday flights, who offer each other sweeties from a bag the whole way. The first soon after sitting down, then another *before* the one they need to save their ears during take-off. Insidious contributors to each others' spongy, spilling girths. Most often it's her offering him, Mummy and wee boy. Eugh. That they could have a sex life, God forbid. Sheridan refuses to think about their fumblings.

She's decided she's like the kid who is new to riding a trike, only able to steer in the direction she's looking, thus veering into the object she's trying to avoid. She keeps steering towards the guy she's already with because he's in front of her – and wonders if this is due to oxytocin, sloth or an undiagnosed mental disorder. Maybe it's fear keeping her there. Sensing the stride of time. Hearing herself saying, 'WhatsApp,' 'Snapchat' and 'woke' gives her the same feeling she has when people say 'interweb' – a nagging sense that it's annoying and everyone else has moved on. Sheridan's watching herself becoming irrelevant just when she'd got the hang of being young.

At a red traffic signal, two cars sit below the bus window. She's hypnotised by their indicators, blinking in irregular rhythms like cheap Christmas lights. She counts – both cars come into sync every fifth flash. Like her relationship. How can the same partner be just the right fit some days and wrong on all the others?

If this was a black cab not a bus she could put her musings to the driver. She remembers a cabbie telling her that his previous passengers had been a couple ending their marriage right there, analysing the pros and cons of staying together and gradually bringing the driver into the discussion, ultimately asking *him* what they should do.

Sheridan supposed it was as good as asking anyone. No one's ever had the magic answer for her.

He was the same cabbie who told her about an old lady he'd picked up from the supermarket with her shopping bags. After a while the woman changed seats to a fold-down one beside the partition and asked the driver if he'd heard of a bucket list, and proceeded to itemise the sexual experiences she'd never tried and *in all seriousness* inquired if he'd help her fulfil them. "Told the old rocket I was married," he said. "You wouldn't believe what I get asked in this job."

Is this the reason to hang on to Ross? So she isn't soliciting cabbies in her seventies? And getting knocked back.

Ross isn't a bad guy. Maybe he's just too Alpha for her, she'd theorised with her friends this evening as they'd slugged Mojitos and condensed a couple of dozen men they'd known into shorthand: when you first start seeing the Alpha male, he never calls and rarely texts, except at random times that suit him but when you do see him, he pays for cabs, buys dinner, and sits confidently close, so you start thinking he likes you, until you wave him off and five days later you still haven't heard a peep. His driving is gallus verging on reckless, with licence points to match, and his idea of keeping on top of his income tax is 'chase me for it.' The chemistry's off the scale – though if you think the sex is going to be about your needs, think again. You feel sort of manipulated doing everything he tells you to naked, but can't help yourself. You morph into a woman who fakes it because it doesn't matter to him whether you come, as long as you make the right noises. Managing your body hair starts taking up only slightly less time than sleeping. The relationship never looks like it's going anywhere because he doesn't contact you for days, sometimes weeks. You wonder who he's with when he's not with you. And after you talk yourself down off the ledge from feelings of confusion and rejection and decide it's time to move on, there he is, wanting to see you again.

You go skipping back. He'll assert that what you're miffed about is that he's not communicating with you like a woman would (reliably, about feelings, and with emotion) – that what you want is a man who's actually a woman. Maybe he has a point. But to spend the night and then go silent – isn't that just rude? No, he'll say, if you can't handle the possible silence, don't take your clothes off. If you can't enjoy it for what it is, you're better off not doing it.

Is he messing with you? Or being refreshingly honest? You've turned six dates into a relationship. And he's turned six hook-ups into a nice experience he'd like to repeat when he's next in the mood. There are degrees of maleness, you recognise and, weary from it, you ignore his texts till they stop.

You find yourself a Beta man who, from the outset, makes taking the lead your task and over-analyses every joint decision (and every film you watch). He hates stress and unfortunately finds even the most basic things stressful – a job with any responsibility attached, being asked to book travel tickets, or meet a room full of your friends. He takes his time in lovemaking: kissing, sucking, and stroking, even when your bikini line reaches your knees. And he'll spend twenty minutes making the precise repetitive motion required for you to orgasm. You know he's not with anyone when he's not with you and, if he has kids, there's often an acidic ex dictating the terms of access (and therefore his time to spend with you). He cooks rather than buys you dinner, which is fine, he's usually a better cook than you. And he'd manage money carefully if he had any, but doesn't, so when he does take you out (birthdays, pretty much) you order something cheap, like pasta, which you could've had at home.

And that guilt, and the dearth of holidays, and inability to plan any kind of financial future, has you longing for an Alpha partner with cash to spend, even for a weekend – until something Beta Male does makes you remember: the solvent guy can do many things for your comfort but he'll never, for example, walk past the remnants of graffiti on a rusted, dented door and notice it, much less point it out, much less understand that it's beautiful. And Sheridan has only ever fallen in love with that kind of man – the kind who sees it, stops and calls her back to look.

On the lower deck, the only people left are two couples in their late fifties, dressed to show they like looking attractive for each other. A soft leather jacket, a satin wedge heel. Evidence of the embedded downturn – those kinds of couples never used to take a night bus.

She remembers their first date: getting ready to meet the guy with the pale freckles who she hoped liked her too. There were no free tables so they hauled a couple of squat stools to a space near the unlit fireplace and, sitting down, it felt like they were in a play staged in a community centre with no budget for props. Sheridan mimed the action of resting her glass on an invisible table and Ross raised a non-committal smile that left her wondering if he'd got the joke.

"We can see each other's legs," he observed.

As they drank and talked, single moths fluttered from the fireplace and flew straight to Sheridan. Which made her appear to be the Dr. Doolittle of Lepidoptera and they laughed about it. She couldn't admit that she'd been placing clothes-moth traps in her flat before she came out, peeling the protective layer off sticky cards impregnated with female pheromones, and had absently brushed her top perhaps, or not rinsed her hands enough. Either way, she'd acquired traces, triggering a winged exodus from the chimney.

Those moths, it occurs to Sheridan, coming at her like she was their cure, had more of a sex face on them than Ross ever has. As does Nate, emerging from his house to greet her each year. Anytime she and Nate are near each other it's like liquid rushing up a capillary tube. Nothing else is needed but each other for their Christmases, except meals when they feel like eating. No pubs, no box-sets.

Every winter, from early December, she studies weather websites and Ross will say, "Don't worry, I won't drive south if it's too bad." But it's not his journey she's fretting over. "If I'm a day late, I'm a day late," he'll add. (Worst. Possible. Scenario.)

She'd abandon her car and walk to Nate's if that's what the weather dictated. The roads would have to be closed to stop her from setting off (and last year she'd kept going through a whiteout, slowing right down and singing with the hymns on the radio) because if anything happened she had an excuse prepared. It was tissue thin but that was the nature of excuses. A few miles from Nate's was a spa hotel, and she'd tell Ross she'd wanted to treat herself but was embarrassed to admit she was spending her mum's Christmas cash on that, seeing how she was generally skint.

She wants to say it was fate which had brought her and Nate back together; that they'd run into each other. Or that he'd called and said he had to see her, that he couldn't go on sans her. Nothing so Hollywood. She'd messaged him three Christmas mornings ago, after a long lonely Christmas Eve, to ask if it'd be okay to speak. He'd replied that it would. After an hour on the phone they'd fallen into silence, as though they were sharing the same thought, and he'd said, "It can't be me who suggests it. You're living with someone. I think it has to be your idea."

"Shall I get in the car?" she'd asked.

A personal best: bag packed, showered and dressed in thirty minutes. She'd remembered wine, too, and the mini-cheesecakes she'd been saving for her Christmas meal. She'd run back into the house for her phone charger: the only thing that could raise suspicion was Ross not being able to reach her. And with the roads almost to herself, she hadn't known what she was doing – was she leaving Ross? Was she reuniting with Nate? Would she be telling people in the new year, "I moved out, yeah, I'm back with Nate, sudden, yeah, soulmates, I guess."

She'd collapsed onto him when he met her at the car door, leg muscles giving with relief. And for the next day-and-a-half every moment felt doubled in length, but collectively moved at three times their usual speed so, after an eon and a blink, she was putting her bag back in the car. They didn't decide anything. They hadn't talked about it.

Sheridan had chopped an apple into quarters for her car journey. When she opened the folded tissue halfway home and took a bite, she found the garlic from the previous night's dinner prep had seeped into the slices. January was similar: her routine with Ross tainted by the pungency of her time with Nate. But it settled into something manageable by Valentine's Day.

There's a feeling Sheridan covets, that pounces on her sometimes as she's falling asleep, or slinks itself round her collarbone when the lights dim in the cinema, and when the film makes her cry, that feeling keeps her crying – makes her wish she was alone so she could dissolve into chest-wracking wails. But daylight comes and she forgets to act on it, so when it visits the next time she feels worse. What Sheridan wants to feel is absolutely fine the way she is. To feel that her existence is a welcome and sufficient contribution to the world, and her timing is impeccable, like when streetlights flick on as she's walking along, the only one on a dusky pavement – like she can have that effect on her surroundings.

When her contact lenses feel dry Sheridan has thoughts she can use to stimulate tears and that's one of them: the life she should be living instead of this one. But if she and Ross are having a good week, why spoil it, so there are other thoughts on hand for moisture – the three-year-old left to survive on the streets by parents who thought he was the devil; the strangers who assist strangers after a bomb explosion; the scenario where, in forty years, Sheridan might have seen off most of the people she currently knows, yet all of them are healthy now, which means they're lining up into a skittle-strike of deaths, one then another then another, and won't that be more than she can cope with?

Thinking of Nate keeps her going. If she knows she can see him the following Christmas, have three whole days, she can get through. With Nate in her armoury, she's stopped feeling like she's trapped on a traffic island at rush hour.

Even when she's not with Nate, she's with him, but not so that anyone would guess. He's a sea grass billowing in the shallows and she's a seahorse, inches high, with her tendril tail curled tightly around. The observer registers nothing of the tickle and stroke, the tug and side-by-side tie.

If Ross spends his Christmas days with people whom he loves, who give meaning to his existence, why can't Sheridan?

She harbours the fantasy that Ross will set off to see his kids sometime and fail to return – vanish – and how much easier that will make the act of splitting up. Technically, he'd have left her. If he jogs back to a cafe to retrieve an umbrella, or goes to Halfords while she's in Tesco, or goes for a golf lesson on holiday, she imagines him not making it back. Evaporated. Gone.

Before she moved in with him, that fantasy was reversed. She wanted something to happen to *her*, to get the attention of the man who hadn't made up his mind yet. The man she felt might dump her. And if he had, how terrible he'd have felt a week later when a piece of masonry fell on her and her family wept on the news.

What if Ross does find out? What *if*? It's always been Sheridan's view that people who truly fear being caught do not embark on affairs. Cheating is the act of someone hoping to be discovered, a Freudian means to an end. And now that she's in a liaison? Her view has been affirmed. If Ross twigs, the decision will be made for her. Though it's her guess he wouldn't tell her to leave. He'd rationalise it as an impulsive blip redeemable once common sense prevailed. Easier to keep the one you've got.

Nate accepts her being in a relationship because he lives in the moment, though he'd growl if he heard any maxim like that applied to him. Normal rules don't feature: needing to live together, possession by association. If she turns up he's happy. If she doesn't turn up Nate carries on with whatever's occupying him. There's a phrase for that. Non-attachment? And she agrees with it but can't pull it off.

What do couples get together for, if child-rearing isn't in the picture? Company, someone to share feelings of 'love' with, regular sex. The rest is labels slapped on and chains secured. The ego wants to know it's marriageable. The ego wants someone around to cower or pander when it tantrums or sulks. She's as susceptible as anyone – she just wishes these things were named for what they were.

Nate's way is simpler. But harder too because she never really has him. Sheridan knows you can't *have* another human being, but we tell ourselves that we can because the truth is too difficult. Facing the myth of ownership sends people sideways with insecurity.

When they were a couple, Nate wasn't going anywhere but he couldn't promise her that he wouldn't – and she couldn't settle into that. And if she was premenstrual, forget it. She'd make demands he wouldn't yield to, then she'd squawk like a drama-dependent brat. It embarrassed her, that Nate knew she was needy.

Ross lets her hook on. They put their bikes on the car to explore national cycle routes. They take foodie holidays and hold hands at flip-flop pace. He pours two more glasses of wine than necessary and she matches him. They go to gigs. Which helps her make more sense of her break-up with Nate. In the crowd there are two types: the ones who can dance like nobody's watching and the rest, who're watching them doing it. It's rare to become one if you start as the other.

She'd be in bed asleep if a taxi had taken her home. Maybe next year she could splurge on one.

The last step in Sheridan's Christmas routine, after she's back from Nate's, showered and cosy, is to look up ticket websites and book a gig for Ross's birthday. And this year, it has to be at the Barrowland. She'd signed an online petition to save the neighbouring Barrowland Park from developers and wants to experience the artwork before maybe it's gone – the inlaid 'album pathway', a rainbow-striped list of bands that have played the legendary venue.

There'll be an extra part to Ross's present this year. She'll ask him to leave the car in Trongate so they can walk to the old ballroom, and she'll lead him off to the right. And he'll question, firmly, what they're doing in a city park in darkness, but when he sees the bespoke pathway he'll switch to his effusive present-opening response and she'll tolerate it. They'll read aloud the names they're stepping on. And he'll have seen the Beastie Boys back in the day and she'll have been at The Stone Roses, and he'll have seen Jane's Addiction and she'll have seen The Sugar Cubes and please God they'll find at least one gig they both went to, one band they'd had in common before they met, perhaps Portishead, perhaps The Waterboys. She'll pretend if she has to. And she'll let Ross do most of the noticing, the reminiscing. And he'll thank her for suggesting the detour and will stop at the end of the pathway, to bring her in close.

Inside, he'll use his jacket to shelter her from the tumblers of beer and piss flying over the crowd and for one more year, more than likely, they will be okay.

KISSING LYING DOWN

Arriving at the bar half an hour late I point out, "I've ended up looking sort of Russian," and the two of them laugh. The bootleg stretch denims have a dragon design down one thigh, and the silky-knit deep v-neck is fresh wound red. Sexy of a kind, but neither classy nor current. There's a comment from Alison that she'd forgotten how tiny I am.

I'd got dressed in a rush, overtired-but-wired after a week spent packing boxes, moving, then unpacking. I insist on champagne. When have I ever done that? But I've a home to toast. Answerable to no one. And emerging from the subway a moment ago into gilt air, the pavements teeming, it's apparent that while I've been stuck indoors Glasgow's been having a moment: an uncharacteristic hot spell and host to the Commonwealth Games. The bar is wall-to-wall with people making the most.

It's ages since we've managed the same pub on the same night. Pouring. Cheers-ing. There's a bringing-up-to-speed before the conversation turns, as usual, to men. "Can't remember when I last had a third date," Leanne is saying. "They come, they go." She looks deflated.

"At least they come before they go," I offer.

Tipsy on fizz I put it out there, "Maybe not giving away the goodies straight away would make 'em more likely to stick around."

She freezes mid glass-lift. This could be the end of the evening. "If the current methods aren't working," I qualify, "no harm in reconsidering the methods."

Alison piggybacks my courage, "Yeh, make them work a little, so they appreciate it when they get it." And we're all laughing, not because her suggestion was that funny, but because it's obvious to Lianne we've been waiting to say this, and she's left the pit-bull in its cage and allowed us air time.

Lianne sets her glass down. "Fine, bitches. Can I *kiss* someone who buys me dinner?"

"Not for a few months," I tell her, "until you've sussed out if he sees you as a keeper." I am finding myself hilarious.

"If you're worried his interest will dwindle," Alison's saying, "you can get involved in occasional kissing lying down."

"You just told me no sex."

"I know. It's only kissing. But lying down." Which is the stage after upright kissing, according to Alison's gran.

"The risk," I warn, "is that once you've done it no one else will marry you."

The bar's double-door is wide to the tail end of today's heat and second-hand tobacco smoke. We've been sharing opposite ends of a sturdy table with another group of three, but that group has been replaced by a guy with the weekend paper spread in front of him. There's no weighing it up, I simply do what comes naturally and rescue the poor soul –

he can't read a paper on his own, not on a Saturday night. And that's what I tell him, to bring him in, and when it's achieved I glance back, head cocked; *And that, ladies, is how easy it is to meet men.* I excuse myself to the bathroom. When I return a second man has joined him. He hadn't been a poor soul after all, he'd been a guy waiting for a friend.

Our attention is back on ourselves but we don't find our rhythm, can't seem to settle. Alison and Lianne talk towards me while their eyeballs dart. Alison was at the Games' opening ceremony; she's trying to persuade us it was better than it looked on TV. Lianne's having none of it. She'd switched off at the choreographed janitors.

"My dad's a janitor," says newspaper-man.

We haven't been left alone. I pivot to address the neighbour and see that two have become three. A third guy's in the seat to my right. I'm calling bullshit on newspaper-man. "Is that right? Where does he work?" And he's laughing.

Lianne's mid-flow, "...I don't have Tunnocks in the cupboard and I don't country dance."

"Shame," the newest guy replies. "Was going to ask if you wanted to strip... the willow." From his lingering grin I clock 'pished guy' and chuck in, "Anyone notice that they left out a reeling drunk from that jamboree of all things Scotia?"

I don't do wasted and don't care for wasted next to me. Booze alone or Class A side-effects? Or just the way his face works – blank, possibly guarded. One ear's on him, one ear's for the rest of the table. He's been away. He mentions jet lag. He's back to use his vote. He might stick around if Scotland becomes independent but if not, he's off again.

The guy seated on the end is having to work not to be left out. He grabs his chance to play the chivalry card by asking our names, then informing us that he is Keith, the newspaper guy is Sean and the one next to me is, “A total knob”. Here’s a man jockeying for top spot.

Noticing that each guy is wearing a washed-out cotton tee with a faded band logo, I flick my head in Keith’s direction. “What’s going on with the t-shirts – they ironic?”

“*Ironic*? Nope. Is your jumper an antique?”

“I was thinking it looked a bit Russian Brides dot com,” I answer, standing up to display the stretch-denim dragon.

“Right enough... *pre*-glasnost.”

I lean across for a high five, chuckling. I could reel this one in but remind myself that’s not why I’m here. Having just separated, I’m on go-slow in a siding till I’m ready to pick up speed. “S’always a bit hit-and-miss with me,” I explain. “Lianne and Alison have a knack of looking gorgeous all the time.” I’m hoping my friends will jump in and build on this groundwork.

The total knob goes to the bar and returns with a large wine for each of us, which we’d have declined if asked. The last-orders lights flashed already, and who could drink this much wine in fifteen minutes without vomiting in a side-street fifteen minutes after that?

TK offers his glass to clink and I reciprocate with eyes averted, preferring to stay in the general chat. After a couple of minutes I’m sure I’m being looked at, so I turn and mirror his fly-catching face. He doesn’t twig, asking, “What’re you staring at?”

I answer like a ten-year-old, “Not sure, the label’s fallen off.”

Groups have started bustling past our table and a barman’s adding empties to his stack, shouting, “Time up! Drink up!” And in that second there’s a decision to make. Everyone knows it. Who’ll speak first?

"I'll never manage to finish this," says Alison, sipping.

"Bring it with you," says Sean.

"Bring it..." she considers. "Take it, you mean?"

"No, grammar girl, *bring*, we're heading to my place, if you want to join us."

The barman's calling, "Do your talkin while you're walkin, folks!"

"I'm not drunk enough to commit theft," she says, and Keith tells her, "They know him in here. He always brings, takes, whichever, back the empties."

"How far is it?" asks Lianne.

"Yards," TK responds.

It needs only a nano glance between us—*We in? Aye, we're in*—and next thing we're gathering bags and lifting glasses and tripping along the pavement like it's Ibiza '98. And it's not fully dark because in summer, if it's not cloudy, it never hits absolute night. If only Glasgow was like this more often. Too warm for jackets. New people into a gang. Spur of the moment.

We bundle through the tenement's entrance and Sean leads us up the stone stairs. Our words echo in the tiled stairwell and it doesn't occur to me we're waking anyone. Who could be asleep? On the first flight I notice that TK has positioned himself alongside, he is accompanying me up and he bumps an arm against mine. His way of letting me know: claimed.

It bothers me that my response is to feel flattered. *I've decided nothing, Sunshine*. Can't say his chat has impressed. Maybe he'd have talked more if I'd paid any attention.

Lianne and I sit on one leather couch. Alison, Keith and Sean are on the other. TK's plugging his phone into the speakers to get the music sorted. When it's done he takes the seat next to me.

I'm bantering with Keith about bringing women up here all the time, how convenient Sean's place is and how it's not too shabby a place. Keith is changing spot, perching on the arm by Lianne, equipped with what he's about to reveal as his trump card. "Compared to what it was like when Sean bought it," he says, "it's a fucking excellent flat. How much d'you think he paid? Three bedrooms, kitchen, living room. Guess."

If I fancied Keith I'd want him to win this, but I don't. And Lianne isn't fast enough, so I tell him, because I reckon I know. "Ninety-five grand." He looks at me like he'd assumed it would take longer. It seemed obvious, somehow, from the way he asked, and from where we are: it's a nice flat but only because it's had work done. Not a great street. Not something to bid over the odds for in a downturn. He's stuck for how to keep the to-and-fro going and my attention is drawn elsewhere, the music needs a comment. "What is it with guys and Bohemian bloody Rhapsody?"

"If it's a guys' song, why's a burd singing it?"

"That's a woman?"

"Yer maw," quips Sean.

"Naw, *your* ugly maw," TK shoots back, as he walks over to his phone, not that I'd meant for him to check. "S'Pink," he tells us.

"Ah, so, neither of your mothers then." A fart-in-the-wind for gender respect, but something.

Maybe he'll find talking less of an effort if there's only one person to keep up with. I ask what he was doing abroad. He tells me, "Tattoos," and asks if I want one. I examine his slack face for signs of lying and use my instinct. "What were you actually doing?"

Sean answers for him, "Working in a helium balloon factory."

TK adds, "But I didn't want to be spoken to like that anymore, so I left."

Alison cackles. I keep it in. I'm waiting.

"Splitting up with my girlfriend," he says, "then changing my flight so I could visit friends in New Zealand on the way home."

"Nice, you left her to travel back by herself."

"She'd started a job in Australia. I went over to see if I wanted to join her. I didn't."

It happens again with the music: a song I recognise with an unexpected singer. He tells me it's my turn to check. I tell him I don't need to. "Johnny Cash, doing Redemption Song. Odd gems in your phone."

"Brother dumped his collection onto my hard drive. S'a voyage of discovery."

I wish I had something to reach for instead of wine. Alison's conversation drifts into the gap. "Never get too drunk to floss, that's my rule." Party on. I look round to smile at this overheard wisdom and see that Lianne and Keith aren't here. The gang isn't a gang. There's a man and a woman on each couch. That's the pairs decided. I wonder if Lianne's alright. Should I knock the bedroom door for a quick, 'Okay lady?' through the wood? But Alison seems unconcerned and if Keith had dragged Lianne we'd have noticed – maybe she dragged him.

"Who's this then?" TK flicks a finger towards the speakers. "I want to say the Grateful Dead?"

I can tell from his eye contact he wasn't expecting that. "Not just a pretty face," I add, and wink.

"Not even." He laughs too long at his joke.

"A fiver says you've been drinking since yesterday."

"Try Thursday."

"Oh mate," I pout, because if there's one thing guys detest it's pity, "you must hate your life if you need to stay drunk for three days."

He turns to his friend. "Wouldn't be drinking if Sean kept anything better but he's cleaned up."

"Figures. You're the sad case still partying when his friends have gone straight."

And then I become the sad case who starts singing along to a song, regardless of who's within earshot. I've no choice, it's those opening chords. Graceland. The ebullient tone, the skippity pace, and if you're not careful you could think it's a cheerful ditty but the chords are telling you something else, they are clawing at fragile scar lines, and whenever that songs starts up (shop, bar, elevator, wherever) I can never move. I have to stay with that song till it's over.

As I sing TK is silent. Clasped hands on his knees. I wonder if he's taking the piss but he's listening, head tilted towards mine. "She comes back to tell me she's go-one..." The notes ascend, curl and bend over the tappity beat and I don't care who can hear me put feeling behind the words, "Loo-oosing love is like a window in your heart, everybody sees you're blown apart..."

When it ends he shuffles to the edge of the cushion and stands, saying, "You're one of those folk who *wants* to drink for three days but won't give in to it." He goes to his phone. Swipes at the screen. Young Fathers are playing and I'm thinking, *Who doesn't hanker after a litre of gin and a locked door sometimes?* He takes his seat. We spend several quiet seconds failing to find a route back into conversation. He's watching me. "How about moving your hips with the music," is what he says.

"Right. Like I'm going to lap-dance for you." But he's declared intent. He's brought us back to the reason we're all still here. If no- one's phoned a taxi yet, why else?

I haven't lifted my drink from the table since we arrived but I could do with something. "A glass of water would be good," I say. He gets up. So do I. I don't bring my wine to the kitchen.

It's been a long time since I kissed someone who wasn't my ex, and here's this right-in-front-of-me chance to get back on the road of kissing people who aren't him. Somebody has to be the first next person.

I reckon alcohol is making him more confident. Standing in the middle of the kitchen he compliments my lips. His hand is inside my v-neck, massaging over my bra. His other arm is on my back, keeping us close.

"Like my body, too?" I ask. He gives me the answer punctuated by mouth contact, but not eye contact. "Big headed. Full of yourself." He'd started the compliments but is in no mind to keep them going. I lead him to the chairs beside a pine table tucked in the alcove. There's a computer on it. I take the fleece cardigan that's hanging on a chair and chuck it over the monitor, with its built-in camera. He snorts, and I say, "I don't know your pal from Adam. He's not getting a free show for his collection."

We bring our chairs closer, kissing, grabbing at breasts and thighs. I'd loosen something but there are people who could walk in. What a teen party flashback this all is. He makes an attempt to access a breast with his mouth, pulling lace aside to the sound of threads cracking. He doesn't deviate from his mission.

"That's what I get for winching a drunken animal."

"Oh, this is me being nice, darlin. If I was an animal," he says, lifting me onto the table in one movement. The monitor topples.

"Shit!" I laugh and so does he, setting it right.

There's a tap-tap on the door. I regain composure.

"On my way to the bathroom." It's Alison. "Having a nice time you two?"

"Yes. Dropped the kettle. In the sink. All good."

As her heels meet the floorboards he lunges at my neck, presses me half onto the table and unzips my jeans. My hands are inside his t-shirt, touching his damp skin, pushing up material to work my mouth over his chest. And before I can decide whether I'd have gone that far, his hand has worked its way between my pants and my pussy. My wetness deepens our breathing.

"No." I hold his wrist and remove his hand. A little fun, fine, but who wants anything like intimacy with a strung-out stranger?

I sit back down. He lowers his head to my crotch, inhales, brings his face to my neck, gnaws it and works at his own buttons. When he sits up his dick is on display.

"Lick it," he says.

"I don't know where it's been." I laugh.

"Go on."

I put my hand round it instead and he groans as I kiss his mouth. But it's territory I wish I hadn't crossed into so I find a way back, drawing his attention to the voices in the living room. "*Still* talking. How civilised."

"Get on with it," TK hollers, and we're ha-ha-ing.

He guides my gaze downward. I shake my head.

"What d'you want to do then?"

He has a point. Sitting across from one another on dining chairs, at the cluttered end of a tenement kitchen. *Play I Spy?* But I won't be changing my mind. I stayed sober enough to know where I am, and to know what I'm doing. I'm not sucking him off.

I hadn't looked at him directly before. "Got a name?" I ask. I tuck his hair behind his ears to observe his face, because it's an attractive face and I'm just noticing. He doesn't tolerate that. Shakes the hair back out. Fair dos, it must have been slightly mothering.

Now we're standing. I'd gone to the tap for more water, gone for a break from the alcove, and he's pulling at my waistband and we're kissing hard. The sensations of what could be happening flood me – that thing I've given up indefinitely by making myself single. I turn my back to him and lean my forearms on the work surface, reach a hand behind and pull him closer till he locks his pelvis on mine. But he doesn't make more of the opportunity, won't get involved in dry-humping.

"Tease, aren't you?"

I turn around, rest against the cabinets, and he lifts my top, lifts my bra, takes a nipple between his thumb and finger, stretching it as he plucks his fingers off. I link our hands, not wanting to risk a repeat of that sensation.

He presses me against the counter and grabs at the apex of my open zip. "S'not happening," I tell him. "Anyone could walk in."

"What then?" That question. Right now? I'd choose a comfortable seat. To get lazy and have a laugh. It must be after 3am and if we could share a couch, he'd pass out. These bodies haven't slept enough lately and his doesn't know its time zone.

With his weight against mine, his knuckles grazing my pubic hair, he says, "I could if I wanted."

Men have shown me this before. Shown how little purchase I can achieve to shift their bodies away, the strength of their muscles compared to mine. I've hated that sort of play and have growled at them to quit. And because they were boyfriends, they obliged. I've no goodwill in the bank here: I was disdainful of the drunk guy, then chose to take him rather than leave him.

I wriggle away from his hand to fasten my clothes, thinking of something to say that will refocus this. He's walking towards the chairs. Maybe best to phone a cab. He's lifting the keyboard and monitor off the table and setting them on the floor. Making room so we don't have to stand? Wouldn't the chairs be comfier? Then one arm drags hard on the pine table, moving it enough to cover the doorway.

"Just 'cause you've found a way to lock the door I'm not getting naked," I joke.

He approaches with his empty expression. He covers my mouth with his hand and hooks a foot behind mine so I go down in his grip to the floor. He keeps a hand on my face and positions himself astride, shins on my arms. I'm yelling under his palm. Struggling to bite flesh. I can reach his back with my knees but not with any force. When my shoes batter the kitchen floor he moves down to my thighs. The noises I manage to make could be stifled enjoyment.

He tugs and yanks at my waistband with his free hand. It would be easier with both. I'm waiting for him to lift his hand from my face. He knows this.

"S'up to you," he says, "going to stay quiet?"

I nod as well as I can. Panicking for breath.
He shifts his digging fingers off my mouth. Onto my jeans.
Finding a way in. Gripping my throat.
I'm twisting my face away. Mute.
Must keep more men out this room.
"You need this," he's saying, "Naughty girl."

Adm
One

There's much tippity-tap hilarity and innuendo and hinting at meet-ups (and she's surprised how many of them are twenty-two or twenty-five, but there's no harm replying to them because the rest are thirty-six or thirty-nine or forty-three and those are the ones she'll meet first), and then there's an invite for coffee and the coffee doesn't lead to another but that's okay because there are drinks planned with someone else, and then more drinks arranged after the first, easy peasy, but she doesn't stop at that, she keeps chatting with the three who're still replying to her messages, because the other seven went silent, but she couldn't care, some new ones are winking, and the second drink with Darren ends in a snog (and a little bit more but she'll draw a veil), see, she knew the internet would deliver eventually, because it's a numbers game, keep playing long enough, you'll get the goods, and after a couple of days she hasn't heard from Darren but he'll probably get in touch before the weekend, to pencil something, and on Friday she tells herself, *It's not quite the weekend yet,* and by Sunday she's thinking, *There's still a bit of weekend left*, and by Sunday night she's back online and so, she sees, is Darren, but she holds off from sending a *mannerless toad* message (only just: types it out then deletes it) and launches into winking at as many decent and indecent profiles as she can root out, pinging off witty missives to the ones who respond straight away, and when she wakes up on Monday, her alarm is like stabs from the beak of a demented gull.

~

Cupidbullet77:
So?

TwinklingTealight:
La Ti Do?

~

One winks then reveals by message he's reticent about the internet thing. She redrafts her reply from *Pity's sake, man up: d'you think anyone enjoys this barrel scraping?* to *Hi there, how's your day been?*

~

Why narrow the field? A fair chance. That's her policy.

There's no shortage of near-naked selfies (pasty bodies on unkempt bedclothes, in cluttered rooms with psychotic lighting). She holds back from messaging *Expecting a stampede?* Holds it back just in case.

~

HeartMustGoOn:
Hello, how are you this evening?
You sound like a well brought up young lady.
Tell me three things about yourself I don't already know.

TwinklingTealight:
Have I strayed onto Good Christian Singles?

Why hasn't life taken care of this by now? she's asking herself, she's asking her telephone banking teller. A measly snog with a man who threw her back in. The advent of the web was a promise to eradicate solitariness. A vaccine against never having the one. Advertise yourself and take your pick. Yet here she is, email upon email in what should be leisure time. What is the unfairer sex looking for these days? Not what she's offering. What *is* she offering? Fun. Heaps of it. Carefree to the max. Low on dramarama. That's our Chrissy! Do they think she's damaged? Is she coming across as damaged?

Pretending a thing was hers when it wasn't. Rehearsing in her head how she'll introduce her new addition to her friends. Plucking a babe off the internet and having him. Simple. It reminded her of the time she was walking past the Brooklyn pet shop with the pair of caged birds hanging under an awning, like a blue and a yellow bulb in the gloaming, and how she'd looked once, twice, then on tiptoes unhooked their cage and walked down dusk's 6th Avenue swinging it from her fingers, feeling quite the Audrey Hepburn, a doe-eyed sashay past the police precinct, skipping by a busy restaurant's pavement tables, where she'd set the caged birds down beside a couple's meal. Feathering their romance. Perhaps she never actually did, but it makes her think of a time that she could've.

Lying awake, drenched in breath-held excitement with nothing to justify it, except a firm sense that the justification will show itself soon, has its toes at the next corner.

You'vegotmale:
Hello Twinkle,
Made it to the end of your profile. You sound just like me with a vagina!

TwinklingTealight:
Not sure we're too alike, I wouldn't holler "penis!" in a first approach.

If someone isn't looking for her flaws at the outset, it's never going to work. On her next date she will run through her list of defects and downsides early on, get that gnarly stuff out of the way so they can start having fun!

She doesn't feel built for it, rocking home on the subway, studying the intersection between vandalism and restoration, where the removal of graffiti has left wire-wool scrub marks on a metal panel. Sweeps of tight-packed parallel lines, spectral whorls, butter curls, raked Japanese gardens.

If she took steel wool to her tooth enamel would it look like that in nightclub lighting?

EKeasyrider:
Interesting profile. You seem genuine. How would your mates describe you?

TwinklingTealight:
No idea what they'd say, but they hang in there nonetheless. My boredom with this approach is definitely genuine.

Leander looks after his mother in his forties, which just makes him a solid sort, dependable, worth meeting for coffee and a slice. She hears about his more-than-full-time task, about the carer he had to arrange in order to meet. Does that rule him out? No. What rules him out is that he and his brother had married each other's first wives. Divorced, swapped, remarried. And this guy's divorced again but they all take holidays together.

Straight past the door of the loos to the pavement.

When a digital conversation ends without warning Chrissy finds it fun, or possibly vital, to bring it to a conclusion herself. *Yes, Chrissy, I did enjoy our chats.*

-I thought so, Kevin, me too.

-Work's hectic lately, I'm sorry I didn't let you know before I disappeared.

-No problem Kevin, I know you'd have messaged if you weren't so busy.

-Thanks for the time you spent on those messages, Chrissy, when you had other guys you could have been working on.

-I appreciate you realising that was the case, Kevin.

Standing at the park's railings, she sees a guy in business attire brrrr-ing along the pavement on – what *is* that, a kids' toy? It's like a motorised footboard, which barely exceeds walking pace, but to protect himself from g-force he wears a Flash Gordon helmet and wields his briefcase like a balancing aid.

A few feet closer and she recognises him as the man she's agreed to meet. It's reflexive. Primal. Sprinting away as the teenagers she's passing shout, "Get a bike, ya dobber!"

It follows her, toys with her, the sure-as-she's-fit-to-wear-britches feeling that David Lynch is directing her life from a sealed booth in an out-of-town office park.

westend_licker:
I love your taste, I love to give pleasure, I ask nothing in return, if you're interested in a massage, I will accommodate you.

TwinklingTealight:
Make haste with your address and I'll book the Uber!

Neil, the twice daily messager, is taking a holiday with his kid, to his cottage with no WiFi, so they exchange numbers to stay in touch. A call, she presumes. A progression to voices. Days pass with extensive data.

Why is he telling her what albums he listened to while painting the fence? Or that he *was* painting the fence? What use is Huckleberry to her at 200 miles remove? She stops. He's not fourteen. For another two weeks he texts **Hello :)** every few days, adamant he will not make that call. Not that she'd have answered. Though if he'd phoned when she was drunk she might have lowered her voice a few notches and bellowed, "Chrissy's not here, sonny. She's away off interrailing."

What's she supposed to do – sugar coat it?

She has space. A vacancy. An emptiness requiring occupation.

She fancied to open her door one morning and find curated, colour-coded piles of gathered berries and blossoms, left by a male bowerbird, wooing her with his intuitive architecture.

That heatwave last summer, that one candescent week, skin skimming the broiled air and a few folk reclining against logs, dressed to the nines and passing a joint, in the shallow woods of a stately home where a mutual friend was marrying (for the second time; the first time he'd married in a church and Chrissy and Marcus had been there together, engaged, neither of them thirty yet).

The chat was the sparky, collaborative kind—quip, *laugh*, quip, *laugh*—so when Marcus spoke there was little likelihood of anyone overhearing. From head to belly his muscles were saturated with free booze. Red-eye contact wasn't attempted. "It was a mistake," he said in her direction. "Sorry," he said, "for doing that."

It's a sensation like a very old star dying, collapsing to its core before exploding, in the space between her heart and her womb, debris bouncing against the inner boundaries, her solid organs, her hollow ones.

If she can snare one of these lions, these heroes, she'll never end up alone again. Even if it picks its nose and flicks it at her for laughs, she'll hold onto it.

This one hadn't mentioned still living with his parents. Over coffee, she finds out that's a technicality, due to having a mattress, kettle and camping stove in their garden shed.

She pictures the scene: walking an access path round the back and giving his old father a wave at the kitchen window as he stands drying dishes, before entering the shed to have uninsulated sex with his forty-four-year-old child.

She turns, mouthing, *Who said all the good ones were taken?* to the camera that Mr. Lynch surely has trained on her.

~

Comrades_unite:
Got any decent pictures?

TwinklingTealight:
Ah, this old chestnut, 'decent' meaning half-clad because attraction is visual for men, yada yada ...women are attracted to personality which puts us at an impasse, my friend.

~

The guy holds her hand in the street, after their first fumble. Clammy-palmed taker of liberties. And his onslaught of texts. *Calm down*, she wants to respond. In their final conversation (after she runs into him on a date with someone else, someone dressed from Wallis) he says, "Chrissy, I wasn't sure you were ready to be in a relationship."

Clearly he just wanted any girlfriend, fast; and the more like his mother the better. Freak.

~

Her existence is beginning to feel like a teenager doing chores for pocket money. Writing out lines in detention. *Have I done enough yet?* And no one answering.

~

TwinklingTealight:
Don't be a dick all your life, cowboy, and put that thar gun back in its holster.

~

On the brink of giving a damn and damn what the equal and opposite would be. Exerting forces to find out.

~

Horny_monster:
it was u
u reported my photo
they should ban ur photos off here for bein ugly
am back ya witch and am watchin u

~

Block them. Report them. Wonder afterward if they might have been up for meeting.

~

Showing them she's no old-school candyfloss pushover. Putting herself at risk of reprisals. In harm's way. Bringing to mind the evening she'd emerged from the subway, slap-bang into a jittery crowd encircled by squad cars and satellite news vans. An impromptu street party, she learned the next day, for a music legend's early death. But the DJ and dancing had stopped already, so she'd wandered through that unavoidable morass expecting the bullet that would get her next, from whatever madman was causing it all. That moment she'd almost died. She nearly did. She could have.

~

The pain of it. And not sore because she keeps touching it. Sore the way anything essential hurts when it's not supplied. Inadequate air. No food a few hours after the first pang of hunger. What the body does to let its occupant know.

It's why she heaves tears leaning over glass-cased exhibits on Sunday afternoons, or staggers her way up the fruit and veg aisle. Not because she missed breakfast but because she misses the arms that were supposed to have held her as the day began. The smile to share it with on her return.

This agony of biology. Programmed for community and connection. She can't be blamed for not winning on some days, for not being able to endure.

"You get a shitload done, though," a married friend reminds her, "with no bloke, no screaming sprogs." And it's true. Oh, the things she gets done.

~

HungHippo:
Message me sexy girl

TwinklingTealight:
Why have the 2D version when you could have 3D?

HungHippo:
So u want sum of this? Naughty girl

TwinklingTealight:
You could stand to lose a few pounds but at this point, I'll take anything.

HungHippo:
Piss off

TwinklingTealight:
My cat likes to watch, if you're cool with that.

HungHippo:
You need help bitch

TwinklingTealight:
Do I ever! So, so much! And slimline tonic. Just ran out.

She owns active bitch face. She owns we-should-have-worked-through-it face. She owns it-would-have-been-eight-years-old-last-month face.

But she knows she has to love her face before anyone else can. First principles. Prime chapter in the manuals. Good things can't come if she doesn't already love herself exactly as she is.

And the fascists keep asking, "Seeing anyone?" She feels like the only person on the doomed, diesel-fumed earth who understands that the human has a capacity to recover from ripped-open devastation twice, maximum, and after that its tolerance for trauma is all used up. Further heartbreak could be fatal. Voluntarily embarking on another in-love relationship would be Russian roulette. And still they keep at her. "Met anyone yet?"

She shuffles through her flat clutching her open chest together, holding both sides disguised as the flaps of her dressing gown, reminding herself of those people at the Bed-Stuy pool, the poor, poor souls, possibly lobotomised and not a single one there to swim. Slumped on the edge, lower legs submerged and pendulous, tracking her breaststroke with the eyes of the undisturbed.

The woman in full makeup jogging on the spot in the brisk, frisky water, beaming her whole being as Chrissy was passing in the next lane, calling, "Zees is wonderfool eesn't eet? Eet's wonderfool!" *That's one word*, Chrissy'd thought, *that's certainly one word we could use.*

Answering their messages, tippity-tap, ensuring her future as Chrissy-plus-one.

Showing off her nugget and letting others touch it to appreciate its size.

If a mistake couldn't be rectified why admit to making it?

Well, if he's sure, she'd had to tell herself for seven years, *there's nothing I can do.* Turns out Marcus hadn't been sure. Left her to conclude that she hadn't measured up.

~

Perhaps menopause would be the end to the mud-fight of caring about the presence of a significant other. She carries on in the comfort that nature will take care of this.

~

Sometimes Chrissy doesn't mind Sundays by herself. For example, in the National Trust property a few miles from her flat. The elderly couple, both wearing standard-issue earphones with an informative commentary running, and the wife asking (at the volume people speak the first time they wear earphones, before they've learned to compensate), "WHAT EXHIBIT NUMBER ARE YOU ON?" and him answering, "WHAAAAT?"

And again, her asking, "WHAT NUMBER ARE YOU ON?" and him answering, "WHAAAAT?" A conversation that will repeat itself daily wherever it is they call home.

~

Arguably, the "No Poo No Pee" warning sign tacked to the cast iron border of the townhouse garden makes that street-side oasis more unattractive than the poo or pee would. Arguably, pointing out what is wrong with your relationship makes the whole thing less attractive than if you keep your mouth shut. Married people understand this. Separated people do not.

He'd created new life with the art student. The one he'd two-timed Chrissy with (until she'd found their Whatsapp message chain and moved out). Made a five-year-old he sees at weekends, according to the grapevine.

She drops a hankie in the Waterstones café and none of the men at nearby tables picks it up even though it's clean. And linen not tissue. If they won't respond to a handkerchief is it any wonder she's a statistic in an epidemic of one-person households? Any wonder she's a ripe fruit rotting on a branch?

Charting her monthly ups and downs, her slipperiness.

Stamping her foot out ahead of her, to prevent a windblown thing from getting any further away.

A photo of her legs ending in spike-heeled shoes. Bat-Signal. The Pavlovian predictability of their responses. The dullness of this game to be played to get connection; get gametes mingling.

Homebrewed100:
Whereabouts you based, my shift finishes at 11.

Inky symbols wind from his inner wrists to his shoulder crests. Chrissy tries sucking them from his skin, gnawing at them while he's toiling inside her and won't notice but they stay put.

That documentary about the woman who was setting the world record for having sex with the most men in one day. Some without condoms. Pausing for lube-breaks and lunch.

Not a woman enjoying herself, not a feminista appropriating the role of stud, despite her espousals. It was a woman who'd spoken to the filmmakers of being gang-raped years before. A woman on a crude quest to re-establish control.

Disowned by her mother after she discovered her daughter's record-breaking achievement. Orphaned into the bargain and the record was beaten not long after.

There are other ways to make your point, Chrissy is proving.

The target held dead centre in the drone's kill-box screen, each strike taking ten seconds to reach the ground ...SEND... breath on hold through the delay.

She'd never let on she was making him pay, but she was making him pay, the last one she'd tried being a grown-up with, the one after Marcus. When he was reeled in, his furniture hauled and installed, she'd asked him to leave.

Because – doesn't take a genius – how long would it have lasted? She had no number for that and she wasn't altogether comfy not having the facts.

"S'alright for you," she whispers, lips inches from their bald pates, their acned backs, their oxter odours. "Alright for you." Honing her witchy skills as chilled wee-hours air settles in where the duvet doesn't fit.

Watching for parallel lines, spectral blue; picturing soft hair like butter curls.

She's a body popping out from the crowd on the platform, the lone chicken bobbing to the edge, craning an anxious bird-neck leftward, hasty antsy tugs, to check for the overdue train. *S'it visible? S'it on its way? When's it coming? S'it nearly here?*

Even though she knows the rules, knows them up and down. The train will appear when you least expect it. Unexpected trains are the ones that show up.

Things she has been asked after intercourse (*immediately* after):

- "Did you know that 'off-side rule' is said the same in every language?"

- "Those rich cunts heading up to colonise Mars need to live underground 'cause of the radiation. What's the fucking point in that?"

- "If my sister was half my age when I was six – what age is she now, if I'm seventy?"

As she's seeing them off at the front door she likes to say, "Just going to fish the condoms out of the bin and find my syringe." Click.

Teetering on the razor wire between giving a shit and no longer giving a shit, and not caring who can tell. Intending for a microsecond to hold it then no longer holding it. Bringing to mind that time when she chanced upon Mae West's grave in Greenwood Cemetery and jeered, "When I'm bad I'm better, eh Mae? *Heck* yeah! Three times to make sure, Mae, huh?" It's very likely she walked within metres of the headstone during her daunder there; conceivable that she could have let loose, she might have.

WizardSleeves:
MILF!

TwinklingTealight:
That's the plan. Care to assist? And such a sweet profile name; you a children's entertainer or something?

She'd known there were special interest Facebook groups, but that meant involvement could be claimed in future. Plus they were fertilising dozens at a time those guys, and she didn't want her offspring marrying its sibling.

She gets herself round the corner, that's as far as she manages, after witnessing the old lady pushing the shopping trolley loaded with two gigantic see-through bags of litter.

Her knee-high dog, loose leash, taking its cue, stopping when she did. Only desire to fulfil its duty at midnight. Unaware that not all dogs do that, that its tasks weren't typical. Who has to live like that? Why isn't there help for them? Why is she collecting refuse? Where would they sleep?

What events lead to that being a woman's life in her late sixties?

TwinklingTealight:
You, my good man, have the intelligence of a bag.

Kerr-plunk:
No, dearest, YOU have the intelligence of a bag – because I'm assuming you meant 'of a bug' and are misquoting the A.I. theory of Technological Singularity?
Allow me to mansplain?

"Who's the daddy?" he asks her, like a 1970s porn throwback.

"You're the daddy!" she screams through the stream from his showerhead. "You're the daddy!"

The torn ticket stub is there on the bedroom floor in the morning; the piece handed back in case of needing to pee or buy a drink during the performance.

Adm
One

Which she takes as a good omen.

The early summer deluge, the sudden loss of pressure, the colliding atmospheric masses, and Chrissy riding the river of rain round the bend of the road gutter, along with the other crinkled debris returning to life.

To free up memory on her phone, Chrissy's deleting old text threads. But not before tying up some loose ends. Ping. Ping.

- You sent three messages imploring me to call you and when I did, you never answered. I hope you're prepared to comfort your daughter in a couple of years, when this starts happening to her.

- Before we'd ever spoken, you texted a photo of yourself masturbating, captioned 'good morning' with a smiley emoji. You should be nervous. I could do anything with that. Let that be a lesson in politeness and prudence.

- You said our children would be beautiful if they looked like a mix of both of us. Dangling the 'C' word so lightly. Be careful what you wish for. Fingers crossed we can assess their beauty in a few months. Check your phone for updates.

Her daily good deeds, stacking up, one atop the other.

Using a pay-as-you-go mobile from the market.

When he picks up she realises she hadn't decided what to open with. Who answers the phone at 2.13am? She opts not to open with anything. Lets her emotions speak for her. Funnelling through the teensy holes on her mouthpiece.

"Chrissy...? S'going on? Where are you?"

A storm, a blast, a tsunami through those holes.

"You in trouble? S'happening?"

The brick wall she's resting against hurts the bone at the base of her back.

"What kind of life is that for a dog?" she asks him, delivered on the outward hurl of a sob. "Stopping when she stopped. No tension in its lead. She came to a halt. It came to a halt."

Slides shunting along the carousel in her head. Is she relaying them aloud, or forgetting to engage her mouth while watching? Is he still on the other end?

"Why her?" she asks him.

~

A few quizzical looks maybe, but no one called her on it, no one actually said, "Away you go, you're fuckin at it." But if they had she'd have told them, "Hey man, that's crazy. Why would I pretend to be American if I wasn't? What kind of dumbass would do a thing like that?"

~

Ah, so they don't all stay silent, she thinks, her phone flashing with the name of one of this year's men. A tummy rush to see it there, lit up. She answers.

"Aye, eh, so," he says, "they told me I had to let relevant, eh, parties know... 'cause it's some sort of, eh, super strain, that's spreading... but if we used protection you'll likely be okay. Still need to get checked, they said... I, eh, cannae mind, about the condoms, maybe you can."

Indeed. She can.

There'd be one antibiotic left that would cure her and her nugget, surely.

He spent twenty years in prison though he didn't murder anyone. And he describes the social worker who visited him and became a champion for his cause. Their budding friendship. Evolving relationship. So far, so inevitable. Prisoner marries prison visitor.

Then he explains how, for the first time in his thirty-something existence, he came to know what being loved was like, loved simply for who he was. And how this profoundly changed him and his decision to be a better man. After a considered pause, "She felt like home to me", are the words he uses, for what he's experienced.

Chrissy has to rewind the ten or so minutes that follow because she's cried for a while and missed them.

Lowering the laptop lid is like coming indoors from the glare, everything blue and blurred and undefined.

In her dream she was an artist with a basement studio in a grand city relic under refurbishment. Her tenure would last until they got round to renovating the cellar and then she'd be out.

Big-scale pieces were her thing. Over time the contractors got to know what she was doing down there. The electricians and plumbers, plasterers and painters, joiners and fitters took it on themselves to take an interest in her developing works, her methods. They rescued items earmarked for the skip which they thought could be useful, and brought their selections down several flights. Gaining confidence with each offering.

It was where the magic happened, in the comingling of their aesthetics with hers.

That was some heavy persuasion Marcus had piled upon her, to suction out the seedling he'd planted inside Chrissy by accident.

Turning it into that time when she nearly did. That occasion when she could have.

Cradling it. Holding it over the scar line down her sternum. Keeping herself whole for it.

IT'S A MAN I NEED

We would catch other people's cast-offs and take them home with us. Feed them up and make them ours.

The first one I remember was early in our story, our second or third trip out. In a rural mini-mart, a cashier who'd learned English from the locals was having problems with the barcode scanner. He looked at our plastic-wrapped pork pie.

- Eet no gaun, lady. Eet just no gaun.

You squeezed my arm. I had to leave. You came out of the shop and erupted.

'Eet no gaun, lady, eet just no gaun' found its way into our codex, from an over-filled dishwasher to bedroom antics.

It was your habit, appropriating fragments of overheard speech, but it became mine too. Taking on behaviours as a means of endorsing you, of saying, *I want to be yours.*

I steeled myself every time a layer fell away. I'd been used to showing all that there was to someone who decided he didn't want it – who could handle the discomfort as I covered myself, gathered what was mine and left. You hugged each version as she emerged.

On a day that was so much like any other until that point, we'd met; you were making cocktails at your cousin's 30th. Across a table strewn with bottles I'd told you that I didn't see the point of cocktails. Yeah, you'd replied, a lot of folk struggle with that. Your shoulders shook a couple of times before you glanced up from the lime you were slicing, saying, I think the point is to drink two or three. Their merits get clearer. D'you like rum?

In the following months I immersed myself in the culture of us and you got comfy in the space I cleared. This is how we decided to grow old together:

- You'll still shag me when no one else wants to?

- Here, (you held your crooked finger out) pinkie promise.

A pub manager with three-day stubble saying 'pinkie promise' is worth a guffaw. You reddened because you'd said it in earnest, explaining that you'd paid your way through uni supervising kids' clubs. You launched into a girlish name game:

Lara Lara bo bara
Banana fana fo fara
Me my mo mara
Lara!

I woke you up with the same. My brain had worked out the rules during sleep.

William William bo billiam
Banana fana fo filliam

Before me, you said, you couldn't get close to a thing you thought was beautiful. When you'd tried, all that happened was that it became less *it*, and you became less you. Your hand on the Henry Moore in the park spoiled both. Your hand on me changed that.

You were the type to seek and search, to plant seeds then not want what sprouted from them. But you kept wanting me. This is how we decided not to marry:

- It'll be good, both of us living here. (You were tugging at an ear hair you'd located by feel.) Play your cards right and I might let you stay forev—for the duration.

- As your live-in ear hair trimmer.

- Moving in together doesn't... have to mean, eh... not for everyone.

Noticing that I hadn't reacted you carried on.

- Not that you don't need taking in hand, Christ, you do, definitely. I'll make an honest woman of you. Just not, as your...

- Husband? Husband my foot. It's a *man* I need.

I scored big points for that – the first time I'd picked off a bit of someone else's conversation and kept it tucked away until the right moment. A woman talking on her mobile in your pub, when I'd stopped in to say hello. We'd caught eyes but couldn't make more of it. Producing it from my hiding place for our enjoyment made you roar. You reached across, scooping me into your laughter.

We both knew why you'd said it, why you could claim me but not *officially*. We weren't long back from a weekend with your parents, where your father had done nothing without asking permission: Okay if I pop out for the paper? Where shall I sit, here? Where will I put this? Do you want me to lay the table or walk Bouncer?

I don't know what his punishment would have been for non-compliance but he wouldn't have removed himself from his choices if the consequences were small.

It terrified you. *Husband.*

When you realised you were safe on the ringless arrangement, you became cavalier, reinforcing it to make sure I knew you weren't ever going to change your stance. If I was doing something vaguely DIY, like hanging a picture, you'd say, What you need is a husband. A husband'd do that for you.

And I'd say, Husband my foot. It's a *man* I need. Affirming it with an air kiss.

Turning over the soil in the veg patch I'd marked out, you opened an upstairs window, It's a husband you need for that! And I shouted up what you wanted to hear. You knew what I was saying with those purloined words – I didn't want to be asked permission for your every movement, God no. That you might regress to some childlike obedience made me wince. I wanted the person I'd met, not the person I could mould.

Your posture lifted when I spoke, because you heard the truth in the script. *I need a man.* And if it was your day-off, if we didn't have anywhere else to be, I'd add, Know where I could get me one of those? And you'd show me there was one there already.

It could be shocking to others. Hearing us speak that way.

- Can I interest you or your wife in dessert?

- Wife my arse. This here's my woman.

My woman. Like a Spaniard. Mi mujer. I shone as her, because who wants to give up the status of woman to become a wife? Who'd want that?

You didn't need a boss. Or a spouse who stayed only because she'd made vows.

I'm the woman who's stayed twenty-one years because she curled her smallest finger around the hook of yours.

Weren't you right, with your day-at-a-time deal, which has worked so far and continues to, as your days lessen. I'm careful to spare you my thoughts when they blast ahead (how will I manage with you missing?). You have already ruined films for me; taken all the couples on screen and made them us. All the skin explored, all the domesticity, is ours. You're every soldier who doesn't make it home. I'm every woman waiting, grieving.

When friends are feeling brave enough, because it will have been two or three years, they'll say, Why don't you get out there? Start dating. You don't have to be alone.

And your easy laugh will echo, your palm will breeze across my back, and I'll tell them all, Alone? Alone my foot. I've got a man.

FUCKED BUDDIES

"Be a shame to waste this – what are we calling it – tension?"

Was that a wink? She watches to see if Dean does it again. He rests his fork, grabs his bottle, swigs. Laughs. "At this point, doll, I'd say it's inevitable." There. On the table. But with a lightness that can pass as kidology if his offer isn't taken.

"'Course," he's dabbing at stray table crumbs with a finger pad, "you might not want to start into something casual."

How had she become half of this Mills and Boon moment? By sitting late in a café when her kids were with their dad. On Janie's first visit Dean had asked about the book she was reading (actually he'd quoted the Bill Hicks skit, "Watcha readin for?" and she'd adapted the punchline about the waffle waitress to "waffle waiter", just for him). Dean doesn't need permission to speak: if he hadn't been the owner, if he'd just been a punter, he'd have made the same remark.

"An impressive assumption," she tells him. "And who's saying anything about casual?"

"First rule of fuck club."

"Or of Dean."

"Impressive assumption," he mimics. A momentary sensation of where else she could be passes through her: on the sofa, in her onesie, Netflix.

"Commitment is old school," he says, spearing a prawn from her abandoned meal. He wipes his lips. "You should know better than to take length as a sign of quality"—wink—"in relationships."

Should Janie briefly close one eye? What happens after a reciprocated wink – lunging? She wonders if her facial muscles work that way, she'd probably look like there's an itch in her ear canal.

"Small is it? Thanks for the warning." She flings her cold salmon skin onto his plate in case he wants that, too. "Preying on someone at her lowest ebb"—if he can say it all so can she—"classy."

He's holding his phone, swiping its menus. "Preying? Providing. A rebound service. So the heartbroken can move on." A song starts over the café speakers; the plinkety-synth intro to Marvin Gaye's *Sexual Healing*. She laughs, she can't help it.

By her third visit, they'd greeted each other as friends. She'd taken her usual stool at the counter and he'd punctuated his shift with comments to maintain the conversation, and with gestures designed to stop her glancing elsewhere (knuckle across a knee, palm on a shoulder). Sometimes he'd brought her a small dish to taste, until this became what happened on alternate weekends: she'd stay in her seat while he locked up and made them food.

"Controlled doses are that easy?" she asks. "Never find yourself falling in love?"

"Falling in love. Bless you. How are we defining that? Can you measure it? Is there a manual?"

She'd noticed this. His dedication to pronouncements that he thought made him original, provocative even, but only made him sound pubescent: newly in possession of a reasoning brain but not applying it to anything worth the analysis. Wasn't there a climate crisis needing solved?

Janie probes a toothpick into the hard wax of a cold candle. "What if your chemistry turned into more, and you formed a deep connection?" Pointing the toothpick, she says, "You avoid getting involved in anything too good. Sidestep the women you suspect could twist you up, the ones you might fall for."

Dean is stacking their plates.

How to flatter a gal. If Janie could bear to sit in her empty house, she should probably start. He reappears with a baking tray.

"How's *too good* a reason against something?" He's cutting a baklava. "What lady logic is that?"

"Fuck you."

"Vulnerable and sassy. Making yourself more attractive by the nanosecond, Sweet Cheeks."

They didn't always open a beer but tonight they're on their third, because it's her birthday. Her ex had offered to let her keep the kids, "Fair's fair, birthdays are special," suggesting Janie could do the same for him, and she'd denounced the change with a haste – and volume – that caught her off guard. Reluctant to lose her evening with the one friend who has no babysitter to relieve? Or fearful to lose the only night free from her children, who've adapted better than she has and are waiting for her to join them while she bobs at the end of a balloon string, refusing to land.

"Try it. You might like it," Dean says. "No Facebook updates. No fanfare."

"On the contrary. This rose baklava should be trumpeted into the room." Janie tests her winking abilities.

She's been as guilty as Dean, but he doesn't have to know she'd started arriving an hour later on Saturdays so she could have her house tidied and de-cluttered of kids' stuff before heading out.

"D'you keep a mattress in the pantry for these occasions?" she asks.

"Why bother, when I can haul you out by the bins for a go against the wall."

What makes Janie a magnet for men like this? Honest as the day is long but no more devoted for that, leaving her little better off than if she were with a sneak.

"If it's reassurance you need, the age difference doesn't bother me—"

She flings a bottle top at him.

"—I don't mind servicing your forty-two-today body," he grins, "while you get my thirty-something one."

"Thirty-what-was-that? Nine? My prime is upon us. Yours ended ten years ago."

Tempted as she might have been, just for the slow slam of it, he's making it impossible to say yes. If she'd been in this conversation in the aftermath of her husband's exit she might have torn their clothes off – but she'd done those weeks of carnage sober and at home, steadily inflating herself with air.

Not every pairing has to become something, but isn't it nicer to start off wondering whether it might?

"Janie," his voice emerges softer, "I haven't been locking us in every other week waiting for my moment." He lays his fingertips on her hand and her brow rises: *Really*? "I like cooking for you. Your free weekends are my stand-out days in here."

For two or three beats she doesn't react.

If he'd courted her properly maybe she could trust that statement. Meet him half way. Why is it her job to leap first? What isn't her job these days? Would it be so hard to invite her out?

"Darling," she lays her hand on his, "so it's been more than just pump-priming?"

He pulls back, laughing. "Pump-priming. I'll be borrowing that."

"Do 'scuse me and my lady bladder." She doesn't need the bathroom.

The narrow window near the ceiling is aslant and the scent coming through drags on her lungs. September's decay pickling the air. White shirts out of packets and regulation leather lace-ups. The relentless creep of darkness, of giving up, going indoors. Going into their company full-time. Not sending them outside at any opportunity. Building jigsaws on the kitchen table while she's cooking; laying homework out on the rug though they've desks in their rooms; refusing to go to bed until she shouts because, if you're nine years old, a shout is the next best thing to a hug. But she can't mine anything extra from herself. So she parents from several feet away.

Back at the counter she announces, "Home time," pulling keys from her bag.

"You're going to drive?"

She knows what he also knows; if anything more is made of her choice the evening is done.

"Wanna lift?" she asks.

"Ruse to get me back to your place?"

"Non-ruse, to take you to yours."

"You're welcome to join me," he smiles. "You'd need to keep the screaming down though, which won't be easy, trust me, but the flatmate's had enough of being woken at all hours."

"Tempting invite – gagged sex with a skanky tart in shared digs."

Dean turns. Starts locking the till. "Must be nice having an ex paying the mortgage. No need for lodgers. Amen for gender inequality, eh?"

Little is said while Dean attends to the lights and padlocks the shutter.

Janie starts the car and enters the traffic, then says, "Sorry, slight detour," and pulls into the petrol station which houses a mini supermarket. "Kids hid the loo roll again. I was using tissues all day."

"TMI."

She parks near the carwash. "Coming in?" She plays it cheery. "Come on, we'll have a giggly tour up the aisles." Janie demonstrates giggling. "Oopsee. I said up the aisle. Your commitment rash is coming out."

"Depends which aisle we're talking about, Hot Stuff."

She opens the door, saying, "Did I mention your humour is obvious?" Is it bothering her that he's still here? She suggested this lift.

Though she needs one item, Janie scans the shelves in case she might need something else. On a different date, she'd be alert for a treat she could get for him. And she'd be operating at speed. Tonight, the till queue is welcome.

It's the worldliness that doesn't interest her. The way grown-ups get together with everything available to them and none of it appreciated. Share food they'd never heard of in their youth. Have as much alcohol as they want to go with it. Have easy transport to private spaces and no curfews to keep.

She'd rather be sneaking off to meet him under the guise of walking the family dog. Would prefer rationed glimpses in the sodium light of intermittent lampposts, one stolen cigarette passing between them and both too nervous, too sober, too self-aware to kiss, until the last possible moment of saying goodbye, when their stomachs are full of ferrets from the need to get on with it. Smoky saliva and the texture of tongues. Things adults wouldn't notice because it's taken for granted that a first kiss will be closely followed by first sex, and the agonising, anticipatory build up is lost. Just lost.

Janie can hear the person ahead's transaction. "Seven pence? D'you know what, don't bother." And the customer waves away the cashier's plastic bag, producing a black, tissuey dog poo-bag from her anorak pocket, which she fills with items outside Janie's view. The woman departs, with Janie wishing she'd been quicker off the mark to ask her for one. She'd have bought some chocolate hearts in pink foil from the box on the counter, and put them in a poo-bag to give to Dean.

In the car, she dumps her bag behind his seat with a feeling she's being stared at. "What?" she demands.

"Nothing." He's grinning. She won't give him the satisfaction of asking twice. She turns the ignition and tosses loo-roll packet at him.

"Gifts? Oh hon, you're too good to me."

"I nearly brought you chocolates in a dogshit bag," she answers. "Didn't want to spoil you."

"I don't need gifts, you're already the prize."

She's reversing the car in a sure arc and then sweeping into the street.

"You're naturally pretty," Dean's saying, "but it's your independence that's the real turn on."

Janie wonders what he's on about and why it seems familiar.

"You're different," he's saying, "from the others. It's because you know you're high value."

Oh God, she realises at the same moment he produces the CD case from under his thigh.

"You looked in my glove compartment!"

"I have no moral fibre, you knew that when you left me in your car."

He reads the cover, "Blank Him Till He Begs – Five steps to get him back if you're sure he's worth having... Interesting stuff, if you're a gullible moron." Dean presses the CD player that her ex had rigged to the stereo when she'd complained that her new car didn't have one.

Chapter One. When a guy ends your relationship, stop all contact. Let him wonder where you are. Men don't respond to pleading, or reasoning, they respond to your silence.

He presses skip.

Chapter Two. Behave like a prize and you'll make him a believer. He needs to feel like he's winning you back, so be a challenge, let him pursue.

Skip.

Chapter Three. Men expect women to want commitment right away and that scares guys. Give him the impression you're relaxed about timesc—

She kills the volume.

"Ridiculous," he says, "to think people can maintain zero contact when they share children."

"There's an adapted version of 'no contact' for parents,

which— No, not discussing. I think this might actually be humiliating."

He brings out his phone and starts texting.

"Give me directions," she's saying, "we can't be far."

Her phone double-dings and she reaches behind, locates the pouch by feel. Clasps it. Reads: **"Chapter 4. Another relationship is not the solution. A life you love is the solution"... With hot sex aplenty😉😈**

She starts moving her finger on the screen, to ask Dean: **What would you know about relationships? You only do hook-ups.**

"Now you're *texting* while drunk driving?"

"I have to check texts. You have to when you're a parent."

"You don't have to reply to them! Hello-o? Death wish?"

Hello-o.

"It's my birthday, I can do what I want."

Dean's voice is firm, "Seriously, Janie. Put it down." Her fingers open like a mechanical grabber and it drops to her lap.

"You were meant to read that when you got home," he says, "and chuckle. Rub yourself and then fall asleep thinking about sex, with me."

"I fall asleep whenever I think about sex with you." Janie fake shudders. She lets her breath out. "I'm not a gullible moron," she tells him. "Being up front with your hunting techniques is a technique in itself. Oh, I'm so honest, I'm the cheeky charmer. You're not, you're terrified. She did some job on you, whoever she was."

He's putting the CD back in its case.

"Heartbroken at twenty-one, is my guess, and you're still taking it out on the rest of us."

When he speaks, it's quietly, to the passenger window.

"Maybe I just don't rate monogamy. A minority, at best, are happy for the long haul. It's not everyone's end game, Janie. But whatever, all men are bastards, the struggle is real. Aye, I get it."

She's grabs the CD case off his thigh and into her door pocket. "Why shouldn't I want him back? He wasn't in love, he was shagging her. Not a big deal, according to Dean here. And if he comes back home and helps with the heavy lifting then, hey, maybe I'll give you a call for the fun little extras."

Tears are making rapid routes over her jawbone. She's keeping two hands on the wheel for Dean's sake, ignoring the furious tickle on her neck until the car comes to a stop at the lights.

"You won't need to turn if I jump out here," he's suggesting, "save you the bother." He's already landed one Nike on the pavement. "Let me know when you're home, yeah?"

And she might have, if he'd meant it.

THIS IS HOW THEY MET AND HOW THEY LIVED AND HOW IT ENDED

Everyone in town had left their unwanted household items out for the annual collection by the authorities, or by anyone else. People were driving slowly round the streets scoping out what they could take from their neighbours. And him the only numpty with no car, or one of them; a woman browsing close by had wandered up on foot, too. He clocked her sizeable daypack with a Tim Hortons reusable cup in the mesh pocket; serious business, junk hunting. Early 20s, so maybe a car wasn't in her budget. Vegan leather Adidas. Probably didn't approve of cars. What's the eco-footprint of plastic leather production? That was his basic problem with preachy people, it didn't take much probing for their doctrines to collapse. Gordon had an involuntary reaction to people who broadcast symbols of a righteous life. He couldn't resist unleashing a little chaos.

Hovering near the same desk lamp on a garden wall, Gordon lunged for it and sprinted off like an athlete in early newsreel footage; a whoop for good measure. He came to a stop. Maybe he'd caused a young woman to feel unsafe in the street after dark. *Dick move, Gordy.* He jogged back. And offered the lamp. It's pure greed, he told her. My apartment's already got a naked bulb in every room.

She didn't reach for it. Kept her expression non-committal. Sensible lass. His accent, his lack of inhibition. She might be the shyer type. I don't have a desk to put it on, he said. You look clever, so you've definitely got one. Here, have it. He held it between them till she accepted.

Anyone nearby would peg this as a first date from the way his companion was involving her body in her reactions, the head-tilt with the laughter, the exaggerated recoil at a cheeky comment, the Lady Di doe eyes while inquiring into his last relationship. He'd seen *The Bachelor* a few times. Gabby had watched it too, clearly, unless these moves were so ingrained she wasn't conscious of them. Flirting by numbers.

I like you already Gabby. You don't need to perform likeable. If he hadn't drunk three beers he might have thought that, instead of saying it.

That came out wrong, he tried to explain. You've flicked your hair a lot in the last few minutes. Just be yourself. It's actually sexier.

Gabby breathed audibly through her nostrils. I mean, he said, I'm trained to study behaviour, it's my job. Here, there's an exercise we do in rehearsals to shake ourselves off and warm up. We could do it. It'll be a laugh. S'called 'who's at the door?' So think of a character, it could be like, a policeman looking for a suspect, or someone who's car broke down, and then *be* that character. Except you can't speak. Just knock at the door and I've to guess who you are, only from your actions.

Gabby seemed reluctant to give it a go, he forgot that civilians got self-conscious easily. He jumped in, I'll go first. Give me a second to think of someone.

Gabby stepped down from her stool. How's about I *exit* through the door, without speaking of course, and you can guess who I'm pretending to be as I'm leaving.

The next day, his phone flashed with an incoming text, more specifically, a series of texts. What was it with young people that they pressed 'send' at the end of every sentence.

You're not so good at that game, you didn't guess 'woman on a first date in a bar'

It's natural to be nervous when you don't know someone

Same reason you drank twice as much as me

It would be 'actually sexier' if you could tone it down on being yourself

The apology and 'hey there' he sent over the following days were blanked. Another week later, a response arrived. **Saw this and thought of you.** It had a link to a Facebook event called Sober Clubbing, on Friday, in the city. That was a thing? Fucking Canadians. The do-gooding degradation of all that's holy.

They took seats a few feet from the dance floor and sucked on alcohol-free cocktails that cost big bucks apiece. Pure and unforced laughter escaped from Gabby as he sat up straight and held the bowl-shaped glass beside his face with a wide grin, like he was advertising it.

Is this social awkwardness I'm picking up? she asked.

Congratulations. You found my weak spot.

Again, her genuine laughter. Glad someone's enjoying themselves, he said, letting his knee make contact with hers.

Hollow victory, she said, shifting position. I've just realised vodka and dancing aren't meant to be separated.

Gordon didn't like the idea of her feeling uncomfortable. That week of silence still haunted him. If they had two bad outings there wouldn't be a third.

He moved closer, so she would hear him without shouting. I'm not leaving till I've conquered this personal Everest.

She replied with a high five.

Here's how we'll do it, he said. Give it the worst dancing we can, deliberately.

Ha, like when someone in a film is trying to dance as though it's natural. No, no, worse, when they solo dance inside a circle at a bachelor party.

No, when they dance in the bedroom mirror before the big date they've scored with a woman they've liked for ages... Join me if you want to. But I owe you some humiliation.

He set his glass on the table. Gabby didn't follow. He danced with his eyes closed, to make moving under surveillance possible. When he opened them, she was there. If you still fancy me after this, he barked in her ear.

I kinda fancy you *during* this. Her face was like an excited kid. New-couple-in-a-nightclub scene! she shouted, and threw her arms up and shunted towards him, both feet at once, to bump her pelvis against his, then revolved around him like he was a pole, then shimmied her chest in his direction. He started laughing too hard to keep the scene going.

. . .

I wouldn't say this to just any man, Gabby drawled, during a stroll around the memorial park, but I think you could make me hear bells. A line she'd heard on a Dallas rerun apparently – one of J.R. Ewing's feistier conquests giving in despite herself – prompting a flat response from Gordon, Ting-a-ting-a-ting.

An unamused trrr-icycle, Gabby said in reply, mocking his Scottish brogue, which triggered some amusement. He owed her that, after they'd stood outside the cinema earlier trying to decide on a film and he'd turned it into a full-scale political hustings. Was it because he cared about his first choice that much, or was it a hard-wired contrariness he preferred to think he didn't possess, or maybe every dollar counted. Archetypal tight Scot. *Nice one, Gordy*. Holding her hand through the film was his way of admitting he'd been somewhat intense.

Coming made her skin sensitive and the stroke of his mouth sent aftershocks the length of Gabby. She described it to him, before fretting aloud that she was taking too much, more than her share. She still took it, though. Women expected to be treated a certain way over here. It seeped through in their chat and their profiles – he'd reset his location on Tinder when he'd landed in Canada and he was active for a few weeks, until he and Gabby had settled into something.

They weren't seeing each other, they were 'dating'. Who uses that word? Unless you're twelve and American. Dating carried expectations, a protocol. She could whistle if she wanted him to find out what it was and follow it.

. . .

Until he could keep pace with Toronto rents, this forty-street jackpot of an outskirts town was home. Walking by an instant print shop on a trip to the city, Gordon turned and went in, paying fifteen bucks for a t-shirt lettered with, 'Back Off Y'all!' He wore it under his sweatshirt some days, to gird himself against the ambush on his private life which started with him buying a coffee or a carton of milk, and continued, *Enjoy the movie last night? Donna passed you and Gabby outside the theatre*. People at home weren't so brazen. Or maybe they knew they'd be wasting their breath. Apparently, being a teacher at the school made it everyone's business who Gabby spent time with.

She messaged him, **It's hard to get away at lunchtime**

That didn't mean she shouldn't try – breaks were essential. **Employers don't own you**, he reminded her, **never let them think that they do.** He worked five evenings out of seven at the moment; he was making an effort.

Helluva morning hon, she texted. **I'll come as long as I don't have to talk**

Was hoping for that, he pinged.

The greaseproof paper around the vegan sandwich he brought her had 'ssshhh' scribbled in thick Sharpie and when she commented, Très drôle, he put a finger to her lips. She sat closer. He curled her ponytail through his hand.

While Gabby ate they watched guys working on a leafless tree encircled with hazard tape. For the first time he was shown that dead trees weren't felled from the base, in one clean go, like they are in cartoons. They were dismantled piece-after-piece by a man in a cherry-picker, taking it down from the crown: sections of one branch, sections of the next, until no branches remained. Then the trunk was lopped till it was squat, gone.

I'm going to work this into a lesson plan, Gabby said. Something around forests and woodland for next term.

Gordon's mate Dougie owned a holiday house in Greece; an option available to guys with salaries and guys who felt okay exploiting a country in fiscal meltdown. Gordon had been a couple of times, the last trip was Dougie's stag week. Because of the baby, Dougie was offering the hottest months to friends. Gordon mentioned it to Gabby. She worked hard, she deserved a break, and they could visit his mum if they flew to Glasgow for the long-haul leg.

Gabby was straight online researching flights – booking a long weekend at his mum's, then Easyjet to southern Europe, and another night with his mum on the way back. Almost three weeks. Gabby said she'd chip in extra to the spending money because he was making the accommodation possible. Gordon could live with that.

As their departure loomed he looked on Airbnb to see if there was anywhere close to his mum, and cheap enough, to put Gabby in for the weekend. He'd started remembering what women could be like, and the ball-ache when you introduced them. Women who seemed reasonable and sane could change in the company of other women. And they always wanted to make it his business but he'd learned young not to be drawn in. He was dreading it, being pulled in two directions by an arm linked through each of his. Introducing a girlfriend to your mum should be a tea-and-scone exercise, not a four-day weekend.

To her credit, his mother's main concern was not wanting to crowd the couple and making sure that she had the right food in (telling him; I got Joan to ask her cousin what they eat in Canada). They had to heavy-persuade Moira to join them at the Riverside Museum. After dinner Gabby was adamant about clearing up, giving Gordon time alone with his mum. When she rejoined them, progress was made on a jigsaw of the QE2 they'd bought for Moira in the museum shop.

On the second night, under the duvet waiting for his body clock to register bedtime, Gordon was telling Gabby not to expect anything because his tackle didn't work in his mum's house, and she was whispering in his ear, Fuck me now, Gordy, and he was tickling her to get her to shoosh. Trying to laugh quietly was making them laugh more.

Hearing the bog flush sent them silent. They held each other for a while in the borrowed bed and borrowed time zone. Gordon wasn't sure if Gabby had fallen asleep. In a low voice he told her, It's a real shame you couldn't have met my dad. He'd have taken a shine to you. He'd have said you were a wee smasher.

There were only so many times you could watch your girlfriend swimming up and down a pool. Thank Christ for the script he'd put in his luggage, to get his lines committed to memory, all eighty-seven of them. Bringing work on their first holiday had been mentioned with a downturned mouth. The sex was keeping him sane; air on their skin on the terrace enclosed by scented trellis plants. One evening – Gabby washing lettuce leaves and him glancing a pepper under the same tap – she shot, Ten minutes! Half-an-hour! Just half-an-hour without you on top of me!

Turning off the water signalled she felt guilty. She stopped short of being able to face him though, so he gave her the bloody half hour. He walked around in the dark and found himself nearly greeting. Were they overstepping it, attempting three solid weeks? During their siesta sex she'd whispered, You'll take care of me won't you? And again, Will you, take care of me? What had she meant? Help her to come? Be gentle? Or the rest as well: a roof, a car each, children? Gordon hadn't answered.

He could have shut the whole thing down with one 'I love you' but that would have made him a bastard, and you need your own respect before you worry about anyone else's.

Once he'd sussed the public transport options on his phone, they caught a bus to the city and a smaller bus to a mountain town which the internet said hadn't changed much for centuries. It was mid-afternoon when the pneumatic bus doors exhaled them into a wall of humidity. Gordon had to eat. Gabby stopped for a few seconds. He felt the weight of her at the end of the hand he was holding. He wasn't allowed lunch now?

Around four o'clock, after salad and chips and beer, they started strolling up steep, narrow streets in July heat and down again and back up. They were too late for the excavated settlement, which closed at 2pm. Hand-in-hand they emerged from an alley into the old town square. Gordon guided them towards the televised football echoing from a bar. He raised an eyebrow at the threshold, and Gabby didn't object.

The game ended, the bar closed and the last bus had gone. At the dim edge of the public square they discussed their options, dehydrated from sun and alcohol, employing slow and careful words to get them through. Gabby was saying very little, which definitely meant she had a lot to say. He was ready to hurl back, How's it my fault? That was queued up in his mouth.

Grappling for an atmosphere that wasn't this, a holiday that wouldn't be more of this, Gordon spied the sunken, tiled rectangle to their right. Maybe there'd be hell to pay but he'd take his shot at deferring it. Observing himself, knowing, *This is what couples are expected to do in this situation*, he took her hand and led her into the centre. Not that either of them could waltz but he made his best attempt at a correct posture and off they went; Gabby got on board, 'la la'-ing a tune.

Applause rang from an iron balcony above the orange trees, where a shirtless man was making the end of his cigarette burn brighter.

Gordon would apologise in a couple of days. It was easier that way. Why excavate the issue right this second.

Gabby told him that his t-shirt didn't make sense in Greece, adding, If anything, it could be causing offence.

To who? You?

He'd brought four t-shirts and couldn't be relegating any to a suitcase. Who honestly gave a toss what was written on a t-shirt? She shouldn't have started this if she didn't want to see it through. *Y'all* looks American, he argued. People expect Americans to be arrogant. Job done.

. . .

Gordon didn't go on the next vacation. Lack of funds. And a new sales position he couldn't jeopardise. A temporary contract, but work was work. No reason for Gabby to miss her chance to change the backdrop, given that her life was ruled by the school calendar.

In the first week she sent Gordon texts from her trip, when surges of affection seemed to catch her and she was inspired to share them. He liked it. He could picture her cute smile on her side of the phone. There was a time difference; she was already in bed when he got home from work, so he couldn't reply.

None arrived in the second week, he noticed.

He found it on Google, the Scottish Society of Toronto, and typed an email before converting it to a Word document; an envelope seemed more fitting. He explained his situation: a one-year work visa coming to an end which couldn't be renewed because he'd reached the age limit, thirty-five. An actor by training, he'd had some roles with a theatre company and had been covering his overheads with casual jobs. Without a visa he would hit genuine difficulties, not least because of his established relationship with a Canadian teacher. He couldn't afford an immigration lawyer. He leant on words like *sincerely* and *regrettably*.

He pressed print, searching in drawers for an envelope. Folding the letter and writing the address, he laughed into the empty room, recognising that he was 'performing the labour of postage' which, according to an actor in a recent rehearsal was 'fetishised' and no longer part of the everyday.

No wonder he didn't hang out with actors. Gordon deleted the letter from his girlfriend's laptop.

When the reply came, it made no reference to his gallus punt at charity, but it did mention a visa specialist who offered reduced rates to Society members (and enclosed an application to join). The final paragraph suggested that Gordon's accent and theatrical background made him a good fit for addressing the haggis at the Burns' celebration in January, for which they could compensate him.

There was nothing wrong with Christmas except, in the days following, a lurching sensation that he wouldn't choose another Christmas like it – three days at Gabby's parents' in a benevolent, boisterous, bickering group. It was a sensation he hadn't been able to pin down until after the conversation Gabby initiated, at the start of the year, when he worked out he'd been picking up on *her* unease.

I feel like we're two different plants trying to grow in the same pot, Gabby explained, and we'd be better transferring to different pots to... get what we need.

Different pots that live on the same windowsill, Gordon quipped, or plants that divvy up their furniture?

Stop making this harder for me.

Harder for – seriously? You're pruning me out of your life, if I'm understanding the metaphor.

I'm saying, we could both use some space.

How much space?

Enough to figure out what we want.

I've got what I want. I think.

Gabby exhaled hard, like a cartoon grizzly bear.

What? he asked.

. . .

Gordon landed on the cab seat and raised a hand to the men in kilts loitering outside the Holiday Inn. They closed his door and slapped the roof as it pulled away. *Best* night! Best since he got here. Ha, escaping to Canada to get over a break-up and ending up back where he'd started. Ah. So. Fuck. He didn't belong. They weren't his people. Those guys tonight, *they* were his people. Men who spelled whisky with no 'e' and never refused another if it was poured. Aye.

His people. *Time to go home, Gordy boy.*

He opened a blank text, focused his finger on the letters: **A guy finds a lassie to cuddle up to & then she turns it all into hard work. I was in love with you. Why were u never happy? I'm on a see-saw. Dunno whether to turn up at ur house or take this cab to the airport** ...his head lolled onto the window-glass, knackered suddenly, the message forgotten already.

Who would he tap for the airfare back to Scotland at short notice – his mum? The woman who worked nights in a care home and had said it was bloody stupid to go in the first place. The same woman who'd done a turnabout after she met Gabby, astounded no doubt, that someone so good had chosen her daft boy. The guy who kept not getting it right. The guy who missed chances because he relied on the idea there'd be another one. Fuck that for a game of soldiers. His life shouldn't be anyone's business. Jesus Christ.

. . .

Gordon had been trusted to arrange their honeymoon. He guessed this was because his marriage proposal had been so textbook, so *The Bachelor*, that Gabby had felt able to let go of the reins. Her honeymoon deserved to be memorable after she'd sacrificed a big wedding for his visa timescale.

Tramping the wild dunes of a Scottish west coast island, they hadn't seen a soul since they parked the car. The tussocky terrain opened onto a long white stretch. Gabby ran around the white and then ran towards the blue. Knowing Gabby, her clothes would be off any moment and she'd be screaming into that freezing sea. In Greece he'd been jealous that he couldn't swim. Not here.

It took him a minute to reach her. She hurled her voice at the wind, Babe, isn't this the most beautiful damn beach ever?

Fuckin incredible!

Miles of it, deserted!

Aye, great spot for a murder.

Gordon!

He stood behind with his hands inside her pockets as they gazed on the complicated sea surface. It made him glad to know she was happy. Gabby began unzipping her fleece, unbuttoning her trousers.

Going in, crazy Canada lady?

She bundled her clothes onto him to hold. You mind? He held two fingers up at her, and she hung her shoes.

Gordon was spread-eagled in the doorway; his rear arm holding the screen door open, his near arm holding the back door wide.

You joining me or not? he asked.

She hadn't finished marking homework till 9pm and he'd been trying not to fall asleep in front of Netflix. Hunting through kerbside detritus was their thing – the way he and his wife marked the anniversary of when they met. Out they should go.

Won't fit in the car, she told him.

'Course it will.

We have a kitchen table.

This one's going in the garage. For my manly projects.

He told her to hold the car at a steady 10 kmph while he trotted behind to support the protruding end. It felt like she was doing at least 15.

Gordon messaged her, **U nearby?** And he re-sent one from lunchtime, **Level 3, exit the lift sorry *elevator*. Turn right twice. Door says Sound Stage Five. No latecomers policy.**

It was only a page reading, but CBC was recording it for a new-drama showcase. Not long till kick off. He jogged down again to see if Gabby was wandering around lost and pissed off. **Sorry if rush hour's been brutal**, he messaged. He turned his phone off.

You pack the fuckin bag – he chucked it across the bed – if you're so fuckin bothered about what I'm taking.

He wouldn't stand there being spoken to like a six-year-old who couldn't dress himself. Tell me – he upped the ante – I've been wondering, did teaching do it to you, or did you go into teaching because you were already like this?

He slid the wardrobe door along to expose Gabby's side. He took a hanger out. Are you *sure* about this one? he mimicked. He could have stopped. He didn't. If anyone at the wedding gives a serious fuck about what I'm wearing there's something not right with them. Total strangers' opinions don't matter. You missed that memo.

He added a few pairs of boxers and socks to his small stack of jeans and t-shirts. It's not other people who're judging me, *honey*.

Lying in a loose tangle on super king sheets in Vermont, he asked, D'you think your mum would lend us her car?

What for?

I want to show you Lorca's cottage. He spent a summer near here, between the wars.

How far is it?

An hour. Thereabouts.

We've got that thing, that lunch.

The wedding's tomorrow, he reminded her.

There's a pre-wedding lunch.

We'll see these people all day tomorrow.

Mm-hm.

This is our one day to *do* something.

You couldn't have mentioned this cottage when we were planning the trip? Or yesterday, or before we just wasted an hour having sex, this pilgrimage that's so urgent?

The guy was a visionary of Spanish theatre before the Nationalists shot him, at the age I'm at now. I will pay the man my respects.

If it means that much, hon, *you* could borrow my mom's car and go.

Gordon moved his bulk off the bed and went into the bathroom, locking it. That was an unnecessary comment to a guy who couldn't drive.

Gabby wouldn't tread on the front decking of the cottage, but Gordon decided the place looked empty and pulled her by the hand up some steps. He kept hold as they looked at a commemorative plaque screwed to the timber. His voice took on the cadence of Lorca's lines:

I want to cry saying my name
rose, child, and fir on the shore of this lake
to speak truly as a man of blood
killing in myself the mockery and the suggestive power of the word.

He dropped her hand to peel an orange taken from his pocket, then he held out half of the fruit.

No thanks.

You have to. He kept his hand outstretched. Body of Lorca.

She took it and peeled off a segment, her face wincing at the sour juice.

On the drive back he wondered if it had been worth the head-nip to get there, worth making Gabby miss her family's lunch.

Tomorrow, he'd work the room like a social demon. Be a five star conversationalist, and witty, and make a show of bending Gabby backward on the dance floor. A charm offensive so that people would say on their journeys home how lucky Gabby was to have such a great husband.

. . .

He could have conked out after take off, no bother. A stupid amount of wine had been drunk until a stupid hour of the morning, but Mrs. Peppy next to him couldn't go anywhere, even home, without getting hyper. She started a game. A quiz. Like something she might do with the kids during a rainy lunch break.

Okay, so, would you prefer to live in a cramped attic in central Paris, she asked him, *or* a four-bed with a pool two hours from Toronto? *With* a home cinema.

Neither.

You have to pick.

I'd rather live in our house.

Maybe our house has been swallowed by a sinkhole and the only choices are tiny in Paris or statement and soulless.

I know which one you'd pick.

It went on for a couple more rounds, until she asked the question she'd been saving; whether he'd rather star in a top-of-the-ratings soap with shitty dialogue and obscene pay *or* have an acclaimed role in a stage play every couple of years, with unemployment in between.

He eyeballed her. She changed tack. No? 'Nuther one? Would you rather win a luxury holiday for *two* people or win *one* ticket to see Scotland in the world soccer championships?

Obeying an intercom instruction, Gordon slammed his tray-table into its upright position. In his refusal to play along he'd missed his cue to give her something. His bad. Nice of her to make it so personal.

He was too riled to doze. He reached over for the week-ahead TV guide from inside her Sunday newspaper and, borrowing her pen, started circling shows he didn't want to miss in the evening schedules. Goading her into a DEFCON 1 if he was lucky; a clip of Gabby going ballistic that someone from the row behind would film and share on Youtube. He hoped his ink project was making her mad. The last time she'd seen him doing this she'd opened the local weekly freesheet at the jobs page, saying, Circle some of those.

He'd propped her birthday card on the kitchen table. There was no present beside it.

He swallowed, he said, I wasn't sure what you'd like.

It wasn't a lie. He didn't see the point of wasting cash until he'd checked what she wanted.

Gabby was going through the motions, opening the envelope, saying, If this was the extent of it you could have sung Happy Birthday and saved yourself three bucks, hon. The performance continued as she regarded the front; hares, line drawn, bought from an art shop. She read his writing: *Happy Birthday!! Nothing's on fire and no one is in tears – not a bad year so far, Gord x*

Limbs weightless and cold, his mind struggled to know if the item of clothing in the hand should go in the holdall, or stay in the drawer.

He carried the unfastened bag along the hallway, reliant on the filling and falling of weak lung walls. He wasn't aware of her behind him.

KNOCKING THEM BACK

She's looking at the guy who's lifting glasses from her table. At the bar his face had been lost in the shadow of his cap; from this angle Lisa notices creases. She wonders if he owns the place.

"Can I bring you ladies anything else?" The towel he'd used to wipe wet rings from the wood hangs out of his pocket.

"I'll let you know," she tells him. He leaves.

Posters of bands scheduled for the basement line the walls, in date order, meaning that it's someone's job to move each poster along when new gigs are announced. She's imagining the scene – the staff lined up and one pulling the short straw from boss-man's hand – when Mel returns from the bathroom. She fails to ask Lisa about drinks although it's her round. Teeth clamped on a black straw, sucking at dregs, Mel makes it feel like their fortnightly committee meeting (*moving now to agenda item 4*), "Anything happening on the man front?"

"No," Lisa answers. But she'll offer a scrap. "Except crushing on the guy who works at the subway."

"*Crushing*? As in, enjoying the eye candy? Or hoping he'll be on duty when you're leaving your flat?"

"More like, wondering if the ticket counter is sturdy enough to take our weight."

Mel, predictably, is revived. "Lees! Take the bus, why put yourself in harm's way?"

Harm? Lisa wasn't flinging herself off the platform as the train approached; she was just chatting to a bored guy with big hairy fingers. "Yesterday he asked how my uncle was because he'd phoned last week while I was paying. And tonight he said; 'You going out *again*?' He's one ticket away from taking my number."

"That's not flirting, it's a show of concern. How many nights have you been out?"

Lisa starts counting then stops. That question deserves aggravation, not answering. "Check it out," she says, sliding her phone across. "My first sext. Arrived this morning."

Mel rummages for reading glasses. "Who sexts at 9.30am? In fact, who *sexts*... Married, is he? Can only text you from work."

"He's not married. He's twenty-eight, and naked, and thinking of me, like it says. Tap the image, it'll get bigger."

Mel raises her gaze. "What's a twenty-eight-year-old doing in bed at nine thirty? Not only is he too young, he's not gainfully employed."

"He looks pretty busy in the photo."

Mel pushes the phone away. Lisa grabs her friend's glass, empty but for wasted ice-cubes, and gives it a rattle. "'Nuther one?"

At the bar there's no queue and a woman twenty years her

junior asks for Lisa's order while a well-worn synapse fires, telling Lisa it's time to start the party, telling her to order something fun. The guy in the skip-cap is further along, in conversation with a girl wearing a white apron and cradling an orange juice. Her pulled-back hair shines in the light from the gantry. Probably talks to him daily at the end of her shift. Probably hasn't mentioned him to her boyfriend. Probably be an item soon, after a drunken lock-in. The barmaid puts two Seabreezes in front of Lisa, who was expecting them to be blue. Instead they're the colour of sunset in a comic book.

Setting the disappointing drinks in front of Mel, Lisa says, "Wouldn't you think these would be blue?" And Mel replies, "What jeans have you decided on?" It takes Lisa a moment to catch up; Mel's read her replies to the morning sexter. A fiver says she's studied his photo, too.

Self-conscious about seeing this guy again, Lisa momentarily hadn't known who to be. He'd suggested meeting for a drink and she'd decided to bump her plans and offer him Thursday. Then she'd messaged again asking, **What kind of jeans d'you prefer?**

- Low-slung boyfriend

- High-waist-tight-on-the-ass 80s

- Classic Levi

- Skinny

- Cute dress over skinny

Six Whatsapps. No reply.

"So there *is* something happening on the man front," Mel says, pivoting her reading specs to her hairline.

Lisa wriggles around it. "Is twenty-eight a man? Suppose it is. No one acts like a grown-up until their forties." *Sometimes not even then.*

"You only see him as boyish, Lees, 'cause he's so much

younger than you." Mel signals to the toilets again and stands up. Her bladder's been like this since she had kids, although Lisa's days of star jumps in a fitness class are over also. She watches Mel walking away and wonders why they still hang out.

So much younger than her. He's not much younger than Simon was the last time Lisa had seen him... eight years back? And Simon was perfectly ready to settle down.

When Lisa first met the twenty-eight-year-old he'd left town afterwards, on a maintenance contract. His only text when he was away said, **I'll give you a shout next week.**

Lisa hadn't been sure what that meant. Which day would he give her a shout? She'd known she wouldn't be able to see him unless she cancelled something – which she knew she would, as soon as the shout came.

With Mel absent Lisa has a clear view to the barman, who drops his eyeline when hers snags it. It's his job to look around the room, what's her excuse? He's changing the CD. The last time she was in here, it was turntables and a resident DJ. An atmosphere. When the place is this quiet it's hard not to be aware of each other.

His song choice suggests that he's onto her. The lyrics are lamenting the summer now it's suddenly colder; wanting to be young but instead being older; needing a bit of love, taking the offer of a shoulder... There's a chance this Vaccines' track is an empathy nod, with resonance for him too, but Lisa senses it's a setting apart – *just because we're a similar age it doesn't mean we're the same.* He still has his pick. He might work in a bar at forty but he's doing quite nicely from it. Meanwhile, Lisa's afternoon was spent at the STI walk-in service – hours of her life mopping up after ten minutes of intercourse with a near stranger who's given her a shout for more of the same. Walking deeper through some tragic postcode, then waiting to be called. You know you're too old for this, she'd thought, when you're eating crackers at the clap clinic because you've come prepared.

Lisa was nonplussed when the nurse had presented an extra-long cotton bud on a cardboard tray, and a laminated instruction card. The items hadn't spurred Lisa into action so the nurse had to explain it to her. "You do the test yourself."

Lisa felt sure she must have misheard. *Why would I do it, when I'm sitting opposite someone trained to do it?* She thought she said that in her head but apparently hadn't.

"I'm not allowed to do internal swabs," said the nurse who, it was becoming clear, was not a nurse. "But I want you to," Lisa told her. "You have my permission." *Keeping STIs under control should not be left to amateurs, that's what got us into this room in the first place.* Self-service; first supermarket check-outs and now critical infection control.

"It's a new clinic we're running," was the answer she got. "Speeds up waiting times."

"How could me taking my vaginal swab be any quicker than you taking my vaginal swab?" Again, out loud. The woman had shrugged, end of discussion. With a *give it here* fluster, Lisa had lifted the paraphernalia and got started: held the laminated card (repulsive, now she knew what its previous readers had done while holding it) and followed its first instruction to wash her hands (try stopping her). Then she picked up the infested card to read the second instruction (a flaw in the otherwise excellent system). Squatting, sticking it in, twirling it for fifteen seconds. When she was done, the woman who wasn't qualified to hold a cotton bud came around the curtain wielding a syringe, strapped a tight band around Lisa's arm, and stuck a thick needle in, until enough blood flooded a plastic vial. She announced that viruses wouldn't show for up to three months so Lisa would have to return for the definitive HIV test. Lisa left with a number to call and an ID code to punch in for her swab results. Half-a-day she wouldn't get back over a juvenile who'd finished before they'd barely got going.

She'd stocked up on condoms on her way out. Stable door, horse and bolted but still, she'd be insisting from the get-go on Thursday. Might even help him last longer. On the bus back to the office she'd been pinned to her window-seat by a man biting into boiled eggs that he was peeling over a Tupperware. A top day by anyone's standards.

Lisa watches Mel coming back from the loo, wondering, *Any news on the minding-your-own-business front?*

"I should probably head," Mel says. "My alarm's going off in nine hours."

So is Lisa's. "No point in wasting good booze," she tells Mel after a hug, pouring one half-drunk cocktail into the other.

Lisa gives her friend a wave through the window. With almost no customers the space smells of itself, of what's seeped into the floor grain; beer spills, detergent and the distinctive vomit scent of Red Bull.

Either he'll join her or he won't. She might as well sit it out. He doesn't look away this time. Giving the impression that he knows: something happened to make her the kind who remains in a bar when her friend leaves.

So? No one gets this far without at least one thing upending it all, leaving a person clinging to threads for a while until they tie a knot in them and get back moving with both feet. Maybe she'd have been here anyway, alone on a weeknight at last orders. Maybe it's because she was already like this that it happened.

She'd assumed she and Simon would be able to carry on as they had been; didn't realise that a moment's confusion meant nothing could continue as before. She wasn't unwilling to see it from his perspective but hadn't been able to grasp it, so she'd asked him, "What for? What would we be getting married for?"

Simon's eager face had stalled, like the big boat-shaped ride at the Pleasure Beach after the upswing, and then started its descent as he'd registered her question. The open box gaped from his hand.

She could share anything she had, all day long, until they fell asleep, but Lisa hadn't known what she could offer on top. What else was there?

In that second she'd felt like someone was trying to plant a flag; to claim her so that no one else could. But she was a self-governing territory. They both were. *Close the box.*

"I choose you every day," she'd said, sounding like movie dialogue. "I can't choose you *even more*." Floundering. "Help me understand. What is it you think that you're asking?"

Simon's wounded expression had shifted to anger.

For Lisa, a relationship was solid by looking back and realising you'd done it – shared a month, shared another, shared a year, shared two. Saying in advance that you'd stay with someone made it no more likely that you would. The only difference would be the dropped anchor of pre-decided pressure.

They'd declared their good fortune often; *Aren't we lucky? Isn't this good?* Marriage was never mentioned. She hadn't realised that was part of a plan to spring it on her.

If she'd understood she'd lose everything they shared in

the space of a few seconds, would she have answered differently?

The grit in her gullet tells her Simon found someone else to hitch himself to. The ones who are that determined always do.

Lisa waits until the barman is within range and raises her empty drink. “Is there time for one more?”

AND MAYBE IT WILL TURN OUT THAT WAS ENOUGH

If you farmed livestock or worked on a trawler – were someone whose livelihood was closely linked to slaughter, or maybe just a person who cared a little less – your default response would be to let nature take its course. But you're none of these and so your default urge is to help it to live.

A few miles further along the evening coastline, a handful of homes is throwing off a glow. Gulls skirt the air. Other gulls scuttle from you as you walk the sand. One scurries ahead in an arc. Smaller than the rest, feathers mottled brown not white, it has one wing open like it's considering take-off, yet it keeps pacing with its unfolded wing.

One task yesterday had been to deactivate Facebook and Instagram to prevent a static existence – banal snaps being ascribed portent, haircuts and denim growing outmoded. Not for you the fate of previous pioneers; their photographic portraits lying flat in display cases to be ogled by post-industrial idlers.

. . .

You've never had a problem with causing yourself harm (junk food during a hangover, saying yes when you meant no, picking at scabs before they were ready) so, for this reason you know that today will go swimmingly.

This morning, half a dozen emails were retrieved from Drafts, checked over and the delay-send function set to eleven hours. Then you changed the password for your email account to an arbitrary sequence of symbols and digits that you didn't note down. You signed out.

Repeatedly, recently, you've been visualising yourself succeeding, step after step: the long drive, the gullet burn, startling cold, gasp reflex. You'd assumed that was the basic principle of goal psychology: an athlete achieves a personal best by mentally rehearsing their challenge and the sequential actions required to complete it.

The penny drops. It's broken. The wing is sitting open because it cannot close.

Before turning off your laptop you watched a clip on YouTube showing how to wipe a hard drive. You followed the instructions. Any documents that would make matters easier over the following weeks were printed out already, sitting in poly-pockets. The half-spent mortgage would clear itself soon, unless there was a clause in the insurance. You'd never felt sure if it was your flat anyway, or if the bank was just letting you live there.

To help empty the fridge, you had lunch. Then tied the bin bag (which also contained your unwashed laundry; the decadence of that) and gave the houseplants a good drink (there was no shinjū pact with the plants).

A little over a decade from now, you would have found yourself walking home during a sunset so immense, so immersive in its rose-gold synaesthetic surround-sound, that it would've carried you into its glimmering sticky heart and you'd have buckled, momentarily, and needed the big red letterbox to support the fact of you.

The most basic mobile phone you could find in the supermarket came with a modest amount of credit. Without transferring any numbers from your smartphone, you'd selected 'factory settings' and left it in a drawer, putting the primitive handset into your bag, unable to relinquish a phone entirely. Pulling closed the front door brought a settling sensation.

Initial internet research had taken you sideways and offered up a theory that humans are adapted for water because early homo sapiens had spent significant periods connected to shore environments, which explained our greasy water-resistant birthing fluids and capacity to dive for minutes at a time. Discovering this had reinforced that you were making a natural choice. You were going to a place that your body would understand.

. . .

On the passenger seat a small backpack contained a sheet of printed directions for your final destination. There was a seven-hour journey ahead and another hour, give or take, until darkness. The car stereo came alive to Primal Scream.

You'd had to email, if only so they'd know where to retrieve you. What use was leaving a note (or yourself) in your home; for whom to find? A neighbour you'd swapped Christmas cards with one time, after they noticed a smell?

In your early, idle considerations, when you'd thought that deleting social media might feature, you'd been inspired to go for a last root around, typing in the names of people you'd never looked for. The person you'd lost your virginity to. You'd clicked on the thumbnail that looked most like your dalliance (is that the right noun?), showing you the page of a successful American porn actor (is that the right noun?), and had to scrutinise his photographs because, to be honest, you still couldn't quite tell (he did look more like the person you remember than the middle-aged sack of salt in Dundee sharing the name). You'd congratulated the universe on its circular sense of humour as, not long after sharing yourself sexually for the first time, you'd heard from a classmate that the man who hadn't automatically become your boyfriend was skipping college to shag anyone with a pulse who was free during the day (a married pub landlady, a single mum, a pregnant teen). A few weeks later he'd lowered his calf-like lashes and asked to borrow some money until his monthly grant came through, and you'd promptly gone to the cash machine (you had no understanding that you could cut ties with people who treated you badly, having grown up dependent upon them) then you'd never seen him again because he'd spent your money on a coach ticket.

This young one will never get the chance to use those wings. And the other gulls are not paying its plight any attention.

Efforts had long felt low on rewards. Increasingly so. Everything – day in, week out, month in, year out – was your responsibility, your decision, your task. The income; the direct debits; the weekly shop; meal prep; keeping the place clean; air in the tyres; researching the best deals on car insurance, home insurance, broadband, interest rates, utilities; helping the elderly (for all the use you'd been, she'd died anyway); reading the meters; booking a boiler service, car service, dentist, hygienist, haircut, optician, smear, breast check, enough yet? Organising a weekend, scheduling the fun. Not that any of those demands presented impossible hardship but they didn't exactly add up to a vision board, so why not take this decision all on your own, too? This task. Taking care of the rest.

The windscreen wipers slid intermittently to deal with spattering drizzle. Flat-headed hills dominated the windscreen, their lumpen slopes streaked with clumps of bloomless heather, looking like joints of meat after the gravy was poured. While skipping from Primal Scream to the Cocteau Twins (yes, you'd done the solipsistic sift through your music collection for the bands most defining of your decades) the radio interjected. The presenter asked an interviewee, "So, what's next for you?"

"Never think about *next*," he answered. "Just do the thing you're doing. When it's time for next you'll know."

All well and good but what if next had never arrived.

You'd developed, or maybe inherited, a sixth sense for the types who could be at risk and the types who never would be. The homes you'd visited where duvet covers had been fastened so that the buttons were hidden inside the seam (by a person not troubled by the extra time that took, nor what the point was).

It was permissible, you'd observed, to talk briefly and in hazy detail about other people who might have died this way. But not to express a view that it was reasonable.

However, just because previous generations had been unforgiving when their grown-up children cohabited, or had a baby outside wedlock, or kissed someone of the same sex, it didn't mean those adults shouldn't have gone ahead and exercised their rights to do so. You were breaching the fence at another frontier.

It was almost a decade before you'd slept with anyone, after the philanderer. A shaky start could do that to a person.

You'd had to compose the emails so they'd know it wasn't a blip but rather a decision. That you hadn't entered a hormonal storm of peri-menopause and succumbed to a dark place. That you weren't being bullied at work. It wasn't because you'd lost your savings playing bingo online. Wasn't because friends had begun developing auto-immune conditions and tumours. Wasn't because your mum's cousin had done the same thing when he'd got back from The Falklands. And wasn't because of anything you still blamed them for. It was so much simpler, like a job you hadn't enjoyed for a while – if you couldn't find enough reasons to stay, it was time to resign.

In earlier storms the bird must have been blown against something, or could the force of the wind itself break a young wing?

A well-meaning woman, your father's third wife was something of a one trick pony when it came to humour. After asking how you were, her second question was always whether you'd met a nice man yet, then answering your silence with, "Not to worry luvvy, I'll knit you a boyfriend shall I? Ha ha ha!"

Ha ha ha. She could knit herself a step-daughter after the funeral.

Seeing him online – his puffy face, his NHS walking aid – you'd gone back and forth for a couple of days about whether to contact him, to tell him you thought he was selfish. Exploitative. An aggressor. But you hadn't – and weren't sure if that's because you didn't have the courage, or you were too embarrassed to admit what had happened. That you'd let it happen. Ashamed you'd taken part and then waited thirty-three years to mention that you were bothered. That it had hurt, actually.

Or maybe you questioned what could be gained by slamming a mobility-challenged grandfather for his teenage behaviour. Whatever stopped you, you hadn't been impressed with yourself. You were able to stop thinking about it and fall asleep by telling yourself it could be a moot point soon, if you wished.

You'd cross-referenced online maps with your road atlas, noting where to leave the car, where to find the path, where the sand changed to rocks. Into your small pack you'd put two litres of vodka and ankle weights from the sports shop. Plus a head-torch, because if you ended up parking the car in darkness you wouldn't be sitting it out until first light.

The mammalian dive reflex could be honed; the body trained to stay underwater for several minutes, with a much slowed heartbeat and reduced rate of oxygen conversion. You had not practiced in the bath. You'd be relying on your non-honed responses and the keen rate of your pulse, which was familiar from the nights when you'd lain on your stomach waiting for sleep, ear pressed into the pillow, hearing your heart coming back at you from within the trembling tunnels of the mattress springs.

You began to need to pee. You laughed realising you could soak yourself, soak your seat, because surely now there were no rules. But it would make the rest of the day uncomfortable and besides, it was hardly a Bucket List top ten, wetting yourself. You held it, played chicken with your bladder to add edge to your journey. You watched for the next sign for services while pondering why you hadn't made a Bucket List. What *were* the things you'd always wanted to try? Had that contributed to this; forgetting to try new things? Forgetting to want to?

Twelve years hence, a child you would have been related to would've shared his explanation for why squirrels didn't have to go to school every day, like he did, and you'd have welled up for a second or two, thinking of him with no one to tell.

You wanted only enough lung capacity not to panic, and to cover enough distance that a return swim would be impossible.

You imagined your final intake of breath. You'd been imagining it often. A reflexive gulp inward. Empty lungs refilling with something as unsuited as water. You imagined the agony for as long as you could.

Most cars had lights on for the gloomy conditions. You registered a set of headlights dead on, in the near distance. Growing closer. Attempting a *double* overtake? There wouldn't be time. The temptation was strong to face-off with the idiot – not to make your death look like an accident, too late for that with the emails set to detonate – because if you let the car collide with yours, wouldn't that show the driver. People couldn't be let off the hook their whole lives. How would they learn? They were in the wrong, let them deal with the consequences. You were Thelma (or Louise; you forget which).

The front vehicle being overtaken braked sharply, as did you, to enable the over-taker to weave back into lane with a second to spare. Everyone took responsibility for the stupidity to make sure no one died. In the nano-second that your car passed his, you flicked two fingers and tried to eyeball him but he employed the tactic of looking straight ahead to avoid admission of guilt.

Your behaviour was depressing – point-scoring on driving skills through glass.

Get a life, you told yourself, smirking.

It was reasonable to expect that you'd spend a journey such as this doing a reckoning, an inventory of how well you'd conducted yourself and whether there were loose ends. But no need. Everything that was ever expected of you, you'd fulfilled. You had not been letting yourself or anyone else down. Your life was far from a TV mini-series.

Slowing into the side road for the service station you could see that coach-tour season was in full June force. Inside, the services were awash with grey heads. You felt decades younger than these people but doing the arithmetic proved you were not. You joined the queue for the loos and afterwards, paused as you were leaving. It hadn't occurred to you that you'd need another meal but the plan would only happen if you had the energy to match it.

You'd have to eat there rather than pick up a snack because eating while driving was illegal and wouldn't that put a dampener on things, to be pulled over for holding half a sandwich, and then fail to present yourself and your driving licence at a police station within the required seven days, thus becoming a posthumous criminal. Which the local paper would upscale: **Tragic Beach Woman Running From Police.**

As you'd emerged from sleep some weeks ago it dawned, for the first time, that back-passage penetration didn't count as loss of virginity. Not that he'd mentioned anything, so you thought he was making a mistake in the darkness which he would correct at any moment. You hadn't wanted to embarrass him by pointing out his lack of basic knowledge. You hadn't known you could speak during sex because you had no experience of sex. Or of speaking up generally. Or of how uncomfortable it would be for days afterwards.

Have gulls no strategy for mending their own? What are this wee thing's chances?

Walking towards the exit you passed a cabinet of refrigerated drinks and wondered whether you should grab a bottle of water for the remaining hours. So you did.

You didn't screech out of the car park like the bandit you were but you checked your rearview mirror a few times. You were a common thief and you'd have to live with that for the rest of your life (figures of speech had acquired an amusing dimension).

Back in the flow of single file traffic, you didn't intend to get sentimental but it showed up anyway – you'd eaten your ultimate meal. Shuffling along the cafeteria queue you hadn't been thinking LAST SUPPER, hadn't piled calorific treats onto your tray, just leek and potato soup carried to the nearest table, and the person who'd served you had forgotten your ration of butter.

You had your reasons why fifty-one years were sufficient and that had been the gist of the emails: *Don't torment yourselves with what you could have done differently, this isn't an escape from something specific or an ending of anguish, it's what I'm choosing and the prospect gives me great peace, so this is not an apology either. Thank you for the good times* (careful not to spell those out, better to let them think that there were some) *and for not dwelling on this.*

Other people's experience of being alive must feel to them like they're torches lined up, ablaze along the ramparts. It must because otherwise why would they hang about? (Although you'd walked past new-build blocks with cat climbing-frames blocking the front glass and flat-screen slabs screwed to the walls, and you'd suspected that maybe, it did not.)

Your father's third wife always insisted on her Christmas Day tradition (if two years counted as a tradition) of 'couples photos' – her with your dad, your brothers with their wives, your niece with her girlfriend – inevitably spending several minutes after everyone else had drifted away trying to get the dog to sit still, for you to have your picture taken.

So many degrees of separation stood between that living room, that grouping, and the house you'd grown up in; you could barely comprehend why you were there.

. . .

It was nearly three decades before comments in the online environment had educated you that plenty of men liked to enter womens' bodies by the rectum and therefore *of course* he'd known what he was doing. Had felt entitled to without consultation.

And if you hadn't been able to look after yourself in your own room, perhaps you lacked the skills which others possessed to cultivate a nest; a haven.

Trees thinned out along the roadside revealing a half-hexagon footbridge over rail tracks and a white-painted station house and, moments later, you caught up with three moving carriages which had recently left the station. You kept pace with the train, lit from the inside, occupied in seats of two or four travellers, people lost in phone screens, all of whom would be gone within a hundred years. Some within ten. A couple sooner than that.

Nobody was ending up anywhere but dead.

And it wasn't anyone's job to search for you, public services were underfunded enough. So in four hours they'd know where you were, if they picked up email at 9pm on weekends.

Forest resumed at road level. Hulking mountain outlines in shades of slate and graphite sat like jurors. A lick of light, blue-ish white, cut into the dusk. A quarter-mile later another flash inside low cloud – whap! Like something was wanting through, something trying to force a hole in the fabric. And the brutal wind could rip the rest, so a torn sheaf of sky and hill would spill over on itself, like the visible world was a painted backdrop and the scenery would be hanging half-off, to reveal—

. . .

You'd remembered someone mentioning that Facebook had a hidden messages function, a second mailbox that you hadn't known about and, as soon as you could, you'd tried to locate it and check.

Nothing was waiting. There was no parallel life where surprise mails arrived with thrilling content. If you were honest, you'd sort of known that before you'd looked.

It came down in torrents and the traffic slowed to thirty. Sloshes of water rose to window level as you coursed the sloping camber. Inevitable, maybe, that the journey would go like this. Biblically raging and thrashing. Testing your resolve to carry on.

This baby gull is not your problem. Absolutely. Is not yours. You have no veterinary knowledge. You have plans.

An onset of hailstones engulfed you in white noise save for the thump of wipers on hyper mode. In June. *It won't work, God mate.*

You'd lain there a few weeks back as the light began to creep around the curtains, not knowing whether to be more upset by the fact you'd basically paid a guy who'd violated you, or that you were a virgin until you were 27.

On Facebook you'd seen his adult daughter and hoped she'd never met a teen help-himself-er like her dad.

That you were useful wasn't in doubt. Dare you say it liked, too. But a person could be useful and liked on a Residents' Association committee and still not want to be on the Residents' Association committee.

Who got to decide how many years were enough years? There wasn't a proscribed duration – the time a life lasted was the length of it. It relaxed you, knowing that you weren't obliged to have any further part.

Waiting at the bus stop after college, one of them had spoken up from within the huddle of boy-men scuffling past, "Lorna takes it up the arse!"

It was days before you'd twigged that it wasn't a non-sequitur. And where they'd got their intel from. *Not by choice she doesn't!* you would scream at them, if you had a TARDIS.

Beyond the sign for the last sizeable town the road became quieter and narrowed to single width in some stretches. You passed access tracks to farms and occasional rows of cottages.

You spent the miles testing whether it was possible to push empty space around your skull, through the brain's compact, curling folds.

Last week you'd created a fake Facebook account and messaged him. Your accounts weren't 'friends' so you didn't know if he'd ever have access to the mail. But you hoped so, and hoped he'd answer it then spend the rest of his days waiting for your reply (and fretting that you were about to expose him on a billboard rented in the centre of his town, as described in your message, all the while straining to recall which of the many women you might be).

The light had fallen by another lumen or two.

As listed on your printout, you arrived at a wide verge with space for several cars. You parked and hesitated by the door with your key in your hand, wondering whether to take it with you. How would that help? You decided to treat it like a hired car and tucked the key behind a tyre.

A grassy path ended at the beach where a heavy breeze was moving wisps of fore cloud at a clip past weightier back cloud.

It was a relief to be there. Arriving on the sand was like walking down the aeroplane steps at the start of a holiday, anticipating the liberated bliss.

One night near your sixtieth birthday your phone would have rung at 2.47am and the twenty-year-old daughter of a friend (who'd died of an aneurysm the previous year) would barely be able to articulate why she was crying. You'd have done your best to calm her and asked if she was in immediate danger. You'd have told her to send you her location, asked if she could see a 24-hour shop or petrol station, and kept her on speaker-phone as you'd dressed. And you'd have said *sorry sorry sorry sorry* to your fifty-one-year-old self, your eighteen-year-old self, as you'd driven through the street-lit city to reach her.

It's tugging on you – the knowledge that there's a chance it could live if someone who knew about these things could attend to it. But who would ever know if you phoned for help or if you didn't? Your conscience will run out in twenty minutes. You do not have to care about this.

Hobbling with its useless limb. It knows something is hurting. It doesn't know why. You can watch its pain but you cannot watch its inability to take care of the pain.

Like the saucepan seen on the hob after you think you've finished washing dishes, it appears that your duties aren't quite done. With the pay-as-you-go mobile you call an inquiry service that you'd never normally use because it releases phone numbers for extortionate sums. There's a fleeting curiosity – if you'd lived like this more often, taken trips, spent money like there were no consequences, would you be having a life you currently didn't wish to leave? But answering that is like attempting to go back through a valve.

When you give the animal charity call-handler the bird's location, she asks if she can pass your number to the regional officer on out-of-hours duty. This feels in conflict with the digital disconnection you've spent the past couple of days taking care of. What are you going to do, refuse?

A little after hanging up, your phone rings. The guy recaps the information you'd given to the operator. He asks, "Is there a towel you can put over it?"

You didn't pack a towel. You hadn't planned on getting

back out. You reply, "Wouldn't it waddle around, dragging a towel?"

"Once the towel's over it you can pick it up."

"Why would I pick it up?" The thought of a struggling bird beneath cloth is abhorrent.

"Take it to your house and I'll collect it."

"I'm not staying anywhere I'm… on holiday."

"Is there a box you can put over it and a stone on the box, so I'll see it when I get there?"

"I'd have to look along the beach. Won't it be stressed, trapped under a box?"

"Right enough, I'll bring the bird therapist with me, how's that?" But he speaks before you have time to. "It's an hour for me to get there. It would help to know it's secure."

This is someone's Saturday night you're spoiling. Piss or get off the pot, Lorna, do the man a favour. "I'll see what I can find and call you back."

"If you can, love, the sooner the better, it's nearly dark."

You find a washed-up creel but it's too small and has latticed rope on all sides. Wandering further you find a broken wooden crate and pick it up.

You'd lifted out your tent pegs, one by one, and here you are. *Involved.*

A new thing you find out about yourself in your twilight is that you can run faster than an injured gull. The hurt wing has to be tucked forcibly within the confines of the box and the anguish this causes you both is considerable. You run to the tide line to rinse your fingers of lice that you're sure must be on them.

Shaking water from your hands you're reminded of

something you'd read online, about the portion of sea between shore and horizon being known as the offing. Which means your death is literally in the offing.

You reach for the phone to call the officer back and notice the time. So. Your emails have landed. For sixty-seven minutes people have been party to your decision. Except you'd been aiming for the poetry of them reading the messages while you were committing the act. But as noted, your life isn't a split-screen mini-series.

You return to the road behind the beach to call him with less wind blasting into the mouthpiece. You tell him about the box and the rock.

He's thanking you from a speakerphone, adding, "I've put the beach into my GPS. It's a pretty remote spot you've found, at this time of night. You lost?"

"No. Was going for a swim. I'm an enthusiast...of wild swimming. At night."

"A keen swimmer, with no towel."

You have no answer.

"I'm not sure it's the weather for it. You got someone with you?"

"Uh, I left details at the guest house. I probably won't now, it's rougher than I'd realised. You know what it's like on holiday, spontaneous ideas. There'll be another beach tomorrow, I'm up here for a week, so..."

"Tomorrow sounds more sensible. Better yet, a flight to Greece. Anyway, the quicker I get there, the quicker I get home. Happy days. You take care, angel." He disconnects.

Facing back to the sea there's a deep turquoise swatch

where light squeezing through black cloud glances on choppy crests.

In an hour he'll be at your beach.

Calling you angel.

Maybe you could go on a campaign to injure creatures so you can keep phoning him. Maybe there's a sheep you could kick.

The sea is starting to look like it's being absorbed by the sky. There's barely any light. And your family and friends know. And what would the next decades be like living alongside these people whose first thought every time they saw you would be, "Is she plotting again?" Scanning your eyes for signs.

You're pondering whether there will be long-adapted amphibious humans waiting for you. Under-sea nomads to take you in.

You know, though, that you cannot risk being at the beach when he arrives. And you don't have time to find another beach. It's close to pitch black.

You do not need the sea. You have the vodka.

A man on YouTube had died on a dancefloor, after he was filmed downing a bottle of tequila for a dare. Two bottles of vodka should be ample.

There's an opening in the dyke where a gate has come off its hinges. You turn the car into the field, trundle over the uneven ground and tuck in, close to the wall. Enough to be invisible tonight, though not in the morning.

There's a slice of yellow northern night sitting along the horizon, below the cloud line.

You're typing out a text to leave displayed on your screen. An apology to whoever happens to find you. Battery charge lasts for days in these phones.

You screw the top off the first litre and begin to drink as steadily as you can, given the corrosive slick of every swallow. With each slant of the glass lip you're imagining the nightclub crowd, with bets placed, cheering and chanting you on.

MADE TO BE BROKEN

She lifts her wheelie case over the courtyard's low fence, doing the host's gallantry for him. The taxi driver hadn't taken care of it either, nor at the airport when she'd approached his car and he'd popped open the boot from his seat. Yet she'd pressed an extra note in his hand before he drove into the darkness.

In the lamplight of the villa she has no choice but to stare at her host's face because of his allergy to eye contact. On the Airbnb page he'd looked thirty. Probably was, when the photo was taken. A blue filtered tone from high sunlight. Dipped head, dark glasses. Bare chest. The naked selfie struck her as odd for a business profile but she'd noticed how common it was becoming to present yourself that way. Shona had returned to his listing when she couldn't find anywhere else that matched her flights.

The living room holds an acrid reek of raw garlic. Likely part of a regime that this 40-something imposes rather than enjoys. Like his smile. He back-steps towards the kitchen asking if she'd like water. *No sign-in sheet please, no snacks.*

She's ready for the 11pm bedtime she hasn't met for days. Up until 3am at someone's housewarming. Then up last night with a vegan she'd met at a music festival.

Her host hands her a glass. He heads through an unlit doorway off the living room. His voice is very quiet. Addressing his wife? In bed already?

"Okay, let's make pee pee," he whispers, emerging from the gloom holding the hand of a naked girl, abdomen and bottom protruding in the almost-S of a young child. Shona asks her name. "Klara," he answers. "Three years."

"Hello Klara."

The girl is led up the staircase one-by-one, her head turned sideways at the visitor. "We are so looking forward to having you!!" he'd typed and Shona assumed he was referring to himself and his partner – from his photo and name, a young Scandi couple, immigrants to a sunshine island letting a spare room. His wife hasn't greeted her on arrival, she understands, because there is no wife.

Shona takes in the space: tiled floor, beamed ceiling, sizeable fireplace, dark wood furniture, shuttered windows. Like a traditional Mediterranean home.

With Klara back in bed, it's Shona's turn to be led upstairs. He shows her to the room she's reserved for nine nights and tells her that she's lucky because someone else has the small room tonight but, if anyone needs this big room, which is normally for couples, she'll have to move. Shona will have that fight if the time comes.

Online images showed the apex ceiling which she'd thought was an attic; it was the reason she'd booked, because the top floor to herself was like renting a studio. It's just a bedroom with a high ceiling. The tour ends in the bathroom. Worded on the advert as 'the bathroom upstairs', she'd presumed there was another one downstairs, for the owners. Nope. One bathroom for her, the family, and any stranger staying in the smaller room.

They say goodnight. Closing her door there's no lock and God knows who is tucked-up across the landing. Looking for moveable furniture there's only a plastic chair that wouldn't keep Klara out if she wanted in. But it might make enough noise to wake her. She takes a breath. There's a way to handle this. It might not be what she'd imagined but it's a decent room, in a decent house and she's on holiday. It's fine.

A cistern flush penetrates her sleep, which is interrupted again by pulled-along case wheels. An unknown amount of time later she's roused by voices and kitchen drawers and chair legs on tiles. If she lies still long enough it'll stop. Every family readying to leave a house eventually leaves. The last thing she hears is the drag of the front door. She has no idea what time it is. She could switch her mobile on but that would puncture the membrane separating her from home. There might be messages, might be an internet connection. She's here for a break.

The shutters reveal the sludge-coloured sky matching the clay ground. Pulling on the jeans she'd taken off last night she scans the room for towels. Returning from the bathroom Shona dries her face on the shirt she slept in. Downstairs she pours water from a bottle on the counter. The sink is full of pans and there's nothing obvious for breakfast. No fruit bowl nor breadbin. There's an apple in her hand-luggage. She can find a shop when she's dressed.

Her trainers have been lined up under the sideboard with some others. After lacing them she stands up, eye level with a pair of discarded child's pants on the sideboard, dark with dampness.

She can't look for a shop. She has no key. His house shouldn't be left unlocked. Door ajar, Shona follows a footpath between gable walls and finds a garden. In the corner is a giant paddling pool for grown-ups, except it's empty and bamboo stalks poke through the bottom liner. Is this what he'd meant by having 'a pool'? He'd been emphatic. There were exclamation marks. She remembers them.

She shifts a rain-soaked cushion aside to perch on a lounger and tot things up: dull damp weather, audible early starts, shared facilities, a leaky plastic liner... A bush in the corner rustles and a cat drops out. It springs onto the soggy mattress then onto her lap. She sifts its skinny tail through her hand while telling it her troubles and admiring the old stone windmill in the neighbour's garden. She needs food and drinking water. Maybe new accommodation. From what she could make out through the taxi window, the local houses don't add up to more than a hamlet so the shops will be further. Would he mind if the house isn't locked? The cat leaps off at the sound of glass clattering.

At an open garage, Shona finds her host setting empty bottles upright near his bicycle wheel. "You have a good sleep?" he wants to know. Answering him would put her in danger of over-answering; of firing questions to get the information that any hotel would pre-empt. Where are the towels? How far is the shop? Are you giving me a lift there? Can I sit in the living room or is that your space? Is that heap of torn plastic the pool? Where's my damn door key, it's like being held prisoner.

She can't ask though, can't treat him like staff in his own home. "I have some papers for you," he tells her. He's lifting a string bag from the bike's basket. "We sit down, talk?"

The clouds have begun to thin and the sun driving

through the gaps is hot. He moves a plastic patio set to a sunlit patch and says, “Sit,” while he goes inside. She sweeps water off a couple of chairs with her hand, observes droplets coalescing and sweeps them again. He chooses the wet chair beside her, rather than the dried one opposite. He removes his shirt. “Ahh, I am too much inside at the computer. This is good for the skin.”

On his rain-soaked patio he starts explaining water conservation on an island; short showers, essential laundry, then he moves on to electricity cut-outs, the temperamental internet, how the rain won’t last because it’s September, the house-key system (under the plant pot by the door), the previous guest’s angina attack and whether Shona has any medical conditions. After an hour they’ve shared a plate of grapes and she’s guffawing with her *you’ll-like-this-anecdote* voice – the one she’s been using all summer. This is okay, she’s thinking, we might even hang out a little, this’ll be easy.

Now he’s talking about a horse that’s tied to a rope and how the rope is tied to an empty bucket. Where has he seen this horse? “The animal could walk away,” he says, “but it stays, though its limit is in the mind only.” Oh it’s not an actual horse. “Humans are guilty of this,” is the point he’s sharing. Shona’s nonplussed but doesn’t want her silence to imply that she’s mesmerised. His psychobabble tips her into a full sober-but-might-as-well-act-drunk persona, telling him her year has been crazy for this reason and that reason, how she manages a company that hires out marquees because her boss is off sick with Lyme disease, that she’s not had a weekend off in months, and she’s split from her boyfriend of several years but she’s already met someone and she wasn’t even looking.

“Always life’s way, uh?” he offers, and she nods as if that is her general experience. Which it never has been. Perhaps she's told him about men-in-her-life in case he'd taken his shirt off for her benefit. She changes direction, asking if he's off work today.

"I work here. I look after my daughter. Klara's with me 70% of the time." When she'd messaged last week for directions he'd replied that he was 'driving', saying he'd contact her later (he hadn't). Driving at 9am suggested a car owner who was en route to a job, with a house that would be Shona's during the daytime. Not so. But no point mentioning it. He's the type who'd reply, *To assume makes an ASS out of U and ME, hey?*

"Mi casa, su casa," he's telling her. "You must live as you do at home. Join with the family. We're very comfortable with nakedness here, not like in UK, hey?"

If that's humour it falls between the chairs. And his efforts to bond are making it harder to ask this guy about towels. In his home. So what's Shona doing in it? Well the house was listed on a legitimate website, and she booked at short notice, alone because she was too exhausted to handle company. People holiday like this now. It should feel okay. Instead she feels she's in a scenario she might wake up from with her nightshirt drenched in sweat. She gathers their cups as a means to leave the table.

After she's fetched her daypack and pocketed some euros, he rattles off a sequence of directions, "...past the place of sport and the taverna with the yellow...", expecting her to retain it.

"How about you walk me to the main road, then point to it from there?" He takes her along the unpaved trails of the hamlet between boundary walls draped in pink and purple flowers.

The main road is a one-and-a-half-car-width strip of tarmac running between fields to an elevated town. It's 25 minutes until she finds the glass frontage of the town's only grocer, offering a few varieties of fruit and a couple more of veg. Tins, jars, packets. Tuna, tomatoes, pulses, nuts, olives. Can she buy enough for two or three days *and* carry water? When Shona asks for a basket with the aid of role-play she's told, "No" but the woman is selling melons from a box that's balanced on a basket stack. Shona has to fetch a few items, lay them on the counter, then fetch a few more. She could burst out crying laying down her selections, her sustenance, for all to survey, whilst causing obstruction for people who're popping in for less.

She leaves with a full backpack and a square bottle hanging from each hand. Passing the small sports complex, Shona rests the water on the wall. There's a basketball court, a tennis court and an outdoor pool covered with a tarpaulin. Maybe on Mondays it stays closed.

Semi-wrecked farmhouses dot the acres into the distance. The threat of rain hovers for the entire walk back but it doesn't start until she's indoors.

Shona eats at the table then goes to her room because there's nowhere else, but also because her body dictates it (tender glands, sinus ache). Again, it's the sounds of domesticity that pervade her sleep. Klara's return from nursery. She'd been craving a simple week in a sun-soaked garden with nearby swimming; outdoor nourishment and early nights in her attic suite. Instead? Confined to one room by rain and the Monday-to-Friday routine of total strangers. She might as well have chapped any door back home and asked whoever answered if she could bring her case in and stay for a week.

Shona does Sudoku from a puzzle book left by someone else. Later, she prepares food to the soundtrack of a DVD the girl is watching. Not yet a Spanish toddler's bedtime, though well past it at home. Starting her meal, she soon has to rest her fork and hard swallow the first mouthful to quell a surging sob. It's physical. She misses him. Eight weeks is the longest they've gone without contact. The vegan is an adequate distraction. Or possibly the gateway to a deep depression. She'll find out.

She diverts herself with the induction papers from this morning, left on the table. These rules are unlikely to affect her stay, as she wasn't planning on shouting in the street, or making mobile calls after midnight, or bringing sand indoors (the beach must be over an hour by borrowed bike). She broke the rule about not eating in the bedroom but the apple core was tied in a bag so ants wouldn't smell it.

"Sí," her host repeats over Klara's high whine. Their bedroom door opens and the girl appears, carried by her father. He transports her upstairs and the sound of opened taps follows; water slamming the bath enamel. Intonations of protest rise as the thundering water stops. Her host descends the stairs entering his room. He doesn't re-emerge.

She stops chewing to hear better. There's no noise from the bathroom. Shona can't be sure what's safe but she thinks this probably isn't. She resists sticking her head through his door to ask, "Lost your actual mind?" instead depositing her plate then tiptoeing to her room, leaving the door wide. There's enough water movement, enough singing, to indicate that Klara's status is 'alive'. Until the moment the upstairs falls silent.

Shona counts. Gets to six and bolts across the landing, leans on the wooden frame to peek into the room, sees Klara tracing the seahorses on the shower curtain, sees the bath with only Klara in it – no plastic animals, no containers for filling and emptying, no sponge to make heavy then hold high to watch rivulets drain from its underside. Klara's self-amusement continues with another nursery song (each line delivered by an out-breath-then-in-breath). Shona pulls her head back but isn't able to move away. Aside from the obvious health and safety duty, why wouldn't he want to be part of this; the playfulness, the closeness, the most relaxed time of his daughter's day?

As Klara calls out "Papa" with increasing force Shona retreats to her room. In order to shower, twenty-four hours after landing, she'll have to broach the subject of towels. Cocking his head at her inquiry, her host doesn't miss a beat, doesn't say, "Oh sorry, no towels since you arrived?" He simply crosses the landing to some tall drawers, removes a folded, faded towel and places it on the top. Not the two promised on email. When he's downstairs she helps herself to another.

The house is so quiet that she's sure the occupants have gone. Her shutters open to damp roof tiles and stagnant storm cloud.

During the morning the climbing sun burns through again. Shona gathers what she needs to sit outside and dons a bikini under a sundress. In the garden she lifts a lounger over to the sunniest spot beside a fruiting tree and its fallen crop. When she's settled with her book in the bright heat, it's the holiday she'd hoped for. Her mind caves to quiet.

A woozy buzzing is suddenly closer and she jerks her hand, too late to avert a prick on her throat. The silhouette of a wasp bobs away. Is her windpipe working? For now. She mentally searches her washbag for antihistamines or bite creams, recalling nothing, only a tube of aloe vera in case of sunburn (ha). To apply it she'd have to go back indoors. She drags the recliner away from the fermenting fig buffet and protects the sting from the sun with her opened book. It's after 2pm when Shona rouses. She holds off but when hunger starts gnawing she heads inside, past the soiled knickers, where they're finishing their meal. She would eat in the kitchen if it had seating. She carries her salad to the dining area. Klara, who's started drawing at the coffee table, lifts her materials and brings them over but stays standing. Should Shona attempt to chat with her handful of Spanish? Klara's leaning over Shona's lunch. "Mmmm," she lets out. "I want thees." It's a surprise to hear English. It's said again, "I want thees."

Klara's had her meal. Maybe it's not good to give her more. Not without asking her parent. But he's in his room. Klara's holding the narrow end of a sardine. How many germs live on a paw that spent all morning at nursery? "Hang on." Shona trims the end of the fish, indicating it's okay to take it. Klara smiles with it in her mouth. Shona continues eating.

"I want feesh."

Shona can see how this meal is going to go. And feeding a stranger's kid might be wrong but denying her could be worse. Shona's unfamiliar with Klara's tantrum threshold, and doesn't want him summoned by screams nor to embarrass him for his absence.

To achieve prime position in front of the plate, Klara has worked her way between the table and Shona's thighs and pulled herself on to them. It took two attempts but she managed it. "Speederman," she declares, grinning and reaching for a sardine. Shona can't shoo a child away who would have no idea what the problem is. Equally, she's pretty sure she can't have a stranger find his daughter on her lap when it looks like she was tempted there with morsels.

Shona eats faster, aiming for two mouthfuls to every piece she hands out. They settle into the rhythm of "Mmmm" and "I want thees" and "Okay, just a little".

He steps through the doorway of the room off the living room. "Hey, more lunch for Klara?" he says, stepping up the stairs.

Shona explains, "I wasn't sure if it was okay but she—"

"If she is the problem—"

"No, it's fine."

"Sardines?" He whistles. "Very salty."

Shona doesn't respond because she doesn't register it, still caught in the dilemma of the daughter on the knee. The phrase comes back to her when she's dozing against the drumbeat of rain. *I was trying to eat my lunch, made from the only stuff I could buy within walking distance, while entertaining a kid who was so ravenous it was like you hadn't fed her, to avert a tantrum, while you were elsewhere, though still in hearing distance, and you chastised me because it was too salty for your daughter, who helped herself, making me think she was familiar with sardines? You're welcome, arsehole.*

Shona reads on her bed because, despite being large enough for an armchair, the room doesn't have one. She isn't aware of dropping off but is woken by better light coming through the window. There's no one in the living room when she's getting her shoes. Their door is closed.

Meandering the outskirts of the hamlet a thought

manifests – will the vegan be in touch while she's away? Should she turn her phone on? For a nano-second reality tilts and she's not sure of her place; wasn't she sharing a home with a person she loved? Or is she having casual sex with someone different? Hadn't she been building a future-shaped thing?

It would be engulfing her, all of it, if she wasn't forcing herself out to bars and birthday parties and onto aeroplanes. If they'd been holidaying together, holding hands along these lanes – she'd have spent the trip waiting for the invitation to move herself and her belongings back to his. She knows she would, and pities herself for wanting that from someone who isn't offering. At least wondering if the vegan will message is a diversion from wondering why her ex never has.

Fine drops spatter her face and forearms and she breaks into a jog back up the hill. Untying her shoes, Shona sets them beside the rest and sees the soiled underwear is gone. There's a woman on the sofa looking at Shona. They greet each other. Is this Klara's mother, here to collect her? Shona can hear a DVD.

Her host exits his room and sits close to the woman. Shona gets no eye contact. His casa is no longer her casa. She excuses herself. They're still on the couch when she lays her early dinner on the table.

The woman says something in Spanish and he follows her out without alerting the child. Not Klara's mother then?

It was gradual but is becoming unmissable; the DVD volume is bloody loud. Klara appears from the bedroom. "Papa?"

Shona doesn't know what to tell her.

Klara looks inside the kitchen, "Papa?"

"He isn't far away. What film are you watching?" Klara

gives nothing to this woman who isn't Papa. She returns to the bedroom where loud music starts to compete with the DVD, maybe from the computer or a radio. Shona sits. She can't enter their zone. Nor override the choices of a child on the edge of a meltdown. But she can't let this mayhem go unchecked (house rules! This is louder than shouting into a mobile phone at midnight). "Klara?" she calls. Nothing. "*Klara?*"

If her host was close he'd have come already and she can't abandon a three-year-old to search for him. Shona steps across the boundary into the dim room. Klara is lying on her back on the couch and crying. Shona finds the PC and mutes the volume. The TV remote is in Klara's hand so she's not going to remove it.

This isn't the tardis she'd imagined, not the annexe she hoped the two of them shared. It's a regular double bedroom with a bed, wardrobe, computer desk, sofa, television and just enough space to walk between. This is the sum of Klara's enclosure; sleeping, napping or watching a screen. *Rent out one spare room but give your daughter the other.* "Hey chica," Shona motions an arm. "Come to the table. We can draw a picture together. What shall we draw?" She wants away from his domain with its closed shutters and stale air breached by low light from monitors.

Her stepping out is blocked by him returning. She doesn't avoid his gaze, preferring to watch his reaction to finding her there with his crying child. He simply moves aside so Shona can pass and closes the door behind himself. The volume dies. Shona heads upstairs and leaves them to their evening.

. . .

It's some sight in the morning – dinner dishes sitting on the table plus more things piled in the sink. And the list of rules is staring at her from under a water jug.

2b Leave the kitchen / cooking area / tables clean as you found them. Put Pans / Plates etc. back at the same place. Leave the sink clean and empty! It's no fun to clean the dirt of someone else.

2e We live here TOGETHER so please **CLEAN & ORGANIZE IMMEDIATELY** after meals for social and hygienic purposes. This means Eating Area / Cooking Area / Refrigerator.

Where should she leave this list... on top of the cruddy plates or on the stack of saucepans?

It had rained in the night but it's not raining now. She packs a towel and her bikini. On reaching the municipal pool, the tarpaulin is on and the gates are padlocked. Shona decides to go exploring instead, taking a left onto the town's perimeter road and wandering through the cemetery when she finds the gate open.

When she arrives back they're in the kitchen. They end up making and eating their lunches in tandem. At the table, Klara's attention moves between her eggy bread and Shona's side-salad topped with olives. "I like thees," says Klara picking up a black olive. "Hey," says her dad. Shona doesn't want it, so lets the child keep it.

"I'm never sure how much to say. Whether she'll understand."

"English is common with the kids at the apartment of her mother."

"How many olives are here?" asks Shona, pointing to the dark nuggets around her bowl. "One... two..." and Klara joins in hesitantly, counting together to nine. "Smart lass," says Shona, rewarding her with another olive.

While Klara's napping, Shona reads in the living area for a break from her bedroom. Her need for sleep every few hours has waned. She's restless more than tired. Her host exits his room carrying a glass. Shona catches his eye and apologises for interrupting. "Can I ask a couple of things?" He stops to listen. "The sheet mentions recycling food waste but I'm not sure where to put it." He describes the metal bin under the sink. "And the key for the house, d'you bring that in at night?" He reiterates the system of the key under the plant, which must stay there for guests arriving at later times. "And I couldn't see a washing machine, for clothes. I've been in these jeans since I left home."

"That is three things," he says, flatly, which confuses her, until the penny drops. He tells her almost nothing on arrival, she holds off asking so as not to offend him and now he's offending her, on purpose. She's paying to stay in his home and she's not allowed to ask how it goes around here? Two sheets stapled together suggest he cares very much how things go. She adopts the hotel-guest high ground (he pushed her there, by being a dick) sharing her observation of the local pool being closed on Monday and today. "Can you phone them to check the opening times?"

"One minute," he says, offering her the couch she stood up from. After the call he comes back and reports that the sports facility is closed, the summer season ended on Sunday. Ended? Shona couldn't have been clearer. Her favourite pastime on a holiday is swimming. And he'd typed, "We have swimming!! There is a pool at the end of the road!! Nice pool!! ☺"

She'd thought she'd be spending her days there. What

will she do, carless, in this weather? He's continuing, "Oh, and I just made some laundry." As though he'd asked in advance if she'd wanted to add anything. As if she'd have been happy to put her clothes alongside his.

She's glowering at him, yet holding her tongue because she has to and he knows it. The reality is she needs a good review from him as much as he needs one from her. He has leeway to drop stitches because, what's she going to do, risk her reputation as a good guest on the website by complaining about everything?

"I can show you." She follows him to an outhouse.

When she goes back with her half load, selecting the economy setting, she wonders if she should she leave a euro on top of the detergent box, for effect? Or not even for effect. It's occurring to Shona (from the near-empty fridge, the lack of a car in a rural outpost) that her Airbnb fee isn't extra income. Her stay is the reason they can eat this week. It's not a feeling she's had before in holiday accommodation – keeping a family afloat. Being the tourist whose presence the locals need and resent in equal measure.

He appears to regret his slip of the 'gracious host' mask because he's still in the living room when she enters the house. "You would like tea?" he asks and informs. He pours for them and settles onto a sofa, one ankle resting on the other knee, open-bodied, smiling.

"You know rooibos?" He swings his mug to his mouth. "So good for the immune function. You feel it?" He gives a vigorous grunt. She doesn't feel it, nope.

"I nearly died last year," he says, nodding gently. Before she can find the appropriate way to commiserate, he carries on, "I had to leave to survive. My body said enough of this crazy, crazy woman"—one closed fist taps on his skull—"I was too nice, for too long. I gave her this finger, this finger"—he uncurls one at a time—"in the end, she had me like this..." He holds both hands forward as though shackled at the wrists.

"Klara's mother, you're talking about?"

"Finally I understood"—his thumbs are massaging his horizontal calf—"some people are only happy when they are unhappy. It was not possible to please her. I would die with trying."

Shona lays down her mug. "Sounds like you did the right thing."

"Still she wants to keep her crazy control! Last night, wow, she sends a message to cancel her time with Klara. She can't take her tonight. Because she knows that I have a plan and she wants to make a problem for me." He bounces into a new seating position then reaches for the teapot. "More?"

He's pouring before Shona can refuse. "And I am thinking, shit, I'm here with Klara all the week and now I have to cancel my one night." He's trying to draw her into matching his facial expression; scrunched up, slapped. "It's a long time since I had a nice woman for my life. I think this has a chance, you know."

Shona's put two and two together. "The woman I met yesterday evening?" He's shaking his head, "No," continuing, "I knew today that I will never be free until I decide that I *am*. I sent a message, I said, it doesn't matter. Because inside I feel that. It doesn't matter what she does."

So who was the woman last night? He does not badly for someone who's in a hamlet all week with a tiny kid and a bike for transport.

"It's a different feeling I have. A winner's feeling! I will fix my own situation. Simple. Klara can stay here, at home, where she feels comfortable, she will not notice I'm gone."

Oh. The rooibos agenda writ large. Shona could exclaim, "Genius plan! I'd be delighted. You show that nasty lady who's boss." But she will not spare him the discomfort of asking directly. Of forming the words; that he expects her to spend her holiday childminding his kid so he can hook up with someone he met recently. Had he omitted a rule from his list? 4f? We live here TOGETHER, therefore guests will look after my child at a few hours' notice to facilitate my sex life.

"Klara would be so happy to have this adventure, she loves you!" he squeals. "No Papa to stop the fun, hey?" Still he doesn't formally make the request. *She's three, she loves anyone who pays her attention. Klara doesn't know what's best. That's her parents' job.*

"Your girlfriend can't visit you here?"

"Klara doesn't sleep if she's alone. With three of us, that wouldn't work..."

He has a boundary. Good to know.

Shona finds herself agreeing to be Klara's caretaker out of concern for who he might ask if she declines. Who could be less appropriate than a stranger renting a room in his house for a few days? An ostensibly pleasant woman who arrived via a website is given full access to his daughter. Does he read the news? Appearing nice is a prerequisite. But a barrier sits between them – not friends, not familiar enough to challenge. And where would Shona stay tonight if she insults him at 3pm? Where would Klara stay? It might look like a favour to him but this is a favour to Klara.

"Okay, if she won't sleep alone, you'll have to find me a mattress for your floor."

"Easier to take her upstairs with you, no? If you have to leave the room, wait until she is sleeping."

What would Klara's mum make of this workaround – her daughter in a guest's bed? Would she change her mind and take Klara? The answer to that makes Shona too upset to linger on it.

With his hair in ratty strands from the shower, he secures a padlock on his bedroom door (he doesn't trust Shona with his *stuff*?) then he gives Klara a kiss but keeps his movement onward, pulling a waterproof over his fresh shirt and linen trousers. Shona has to dart out after him. "Is there anything she doesn't eat? What snacks are there?"

"Whatever you can find!" he calls from his bicycle. "I will return for nursery," is audible, then he's out of sight.

The show starts now. Shona walks back in. *Klara has to think this is fine.*

Klara is standing, elbows leaning on the sofa cushion, ankles crossed, hands sort of lost-looking. Shona sits on the other sofa and smiles over at Klara, who reaches for the book that Shona was reading. "Eet yours?" The activity whirring in Klara's brain shows in her eyes. While Shona is deciding against explaining that yes, she's reading the book but it's not hers, it was on the shelf, so actually it's Papa's; the three-year-old has begun running with it around the back of both sofas, forcing from herself an hysterical "haha-HA!". Shona hasn't seen the full-on version of this child yet – is this a kid who'll tire of seeking attention if left to run out of steam, or is she the kind who will take it to another level until she gets acknowledgment with a reprimand?

Shona sees the padlock and realises he's shut them out of

Klara's space too. Her toys, her movies, her clothes. Shona shifts her gaze before Klara has a chance to make the connection. Home-made entertainment then, as much of it as Shona can come up with. And no tenner at the end of the evening like she used to get.

"If you sit here," she pats the cushion, "we can read together. I'll read you the story that's inside the book. Can you see what's on the cover?"

Klara comes to a stop between perpendicular sofas. She understood the question, she just doesn't know the word in English. "Yes, it's a boat. Let's find out what happens to the boat." Shona requests the book with an open hand and Klara says, "Okay." She makes a show of getting comfortable to be read to. And within a minute Klara has taken the book back and opened it at a page in the middle. Her language is Danish, with English words mixed in, and this tale wouldn't make sense in either language but that's irrelevant; Shona is being read to by a child who can't read but isn't letting that get in her way. Klara turns a few pages at once then resumes, sending her voice up and down on different words. Shona chips in, "Is that so?" and "My goodness". She imagines Klara doing exactly this with her teacher at pre-school but, as spontaneously as Klara started, she's stopped, laying the book between them, avoiding eyes. Feeling self-conscious or feeling a naughty impulse, Shona isn't sure. She acts fast. "You hungry?" she asks, "because I am."

There's no DVD for Klara to watch while Shona cooks. "Tonight!" Shona says, "We are the famous chefs of the island! And two important guests are coming for dinner..." Shona points at Klara and herself.

Klara clambers to her feet. "Chefs! Shona y Klara!"

"Yes and we have to make something very delicious."

"Sí," says Klara. "Make deleecious."

There's a stool in the kitchen for Klara to stand on. At the open fridge, Shona extracts items, asking, "Delicious or not delicious?" Anything deemed delicious is placed on the counter. Strategically Shona doesn't offer items that would ruin what's already there. They end up with a basic sauce for pasta. Shona chops the tomatoes and onions. Klara plucks basil leaves from the courtyard, and then throws in salt. Once the sauce is simmering, Shona says, "Now! The restaurant!"

"Restaurante!" Klara says, improving the pronunciation.

In the drawers of the sideboard they find a burgundy tablecloth, placemats, candles and napkins. Klara wants full control of setting them out. Shona lays down an example then goes to grate cheese. When she checks, the table is set for five people but fairly neatly.

After their meal the candles become the big attraction, perhaps predictably if she'd thought more carefully. Klara's on her lap, a position she'd taken halfway through eating.

"Leetle baybee, shhh," Klara says to the flame on the closest candle. It goes out. "No," Klara reprimands, thinking that Shona has blown at it. Shona leans back and lets Klara whisper, "Shhh, shhh, bayb—" and the flame dies on the second one. "No!" she turns and scowls, unaware it's her own breath doing the damage. Klara must be getting tired. Shona doesn't relight it, expecting a fight on her hands but Klara announces, "Pee pee." Shona follows Papa's approach. "Okay, on you go, quick quick."

Shona takes their plates to the sink, rinses them and puts lids on pans, sensing that she shouldn't leave Klara any longer.

Making the most of her first visit, Klara is bouncing on Shona's bed. To show annoyance could make the activity more attractive. "We'll have to find you something to sleep in, eh?" Shona fishes in her rucksack for a skinny t-shirt she's had no use for and Klara lands on her bum and scoots to the side of the bed. Shona sees a moisture mark on the blue bedcover. Sure enough, Klara's skirt has a patch on it too. Shona doesn't want to make the girl self-conscious. "Okay, here's your nightie! You put this on while I make the bed."

She turns the duvet round so the damp will be away from their faces, folds the cover down, shakes out the pillows and looks back around; Klara's not wearing her nightdress, she's naked and standing inside Shona's rucksack, about to topple from instability and giggles. Shona steadies her through their laughter. "Ready for your trip to Scotland? Coming home in my bag, you monkey?"

Shona lifts her, "One, two, three," and passes the vest to her. "Teeth next," she says. They're not in smooth territory of suggestion, compliance, suggestion, compliance. The low voltage crackle haunts the air. Klara wants her quota, the extra recognition that an under-nurtured child needs from every new adult. It remains the Klara show. "Ahhh," she says, softly, picking up a pale silicone earplug from the dresser. "Baybee." She cups it in her small palm and strokes it with a finger. "Baybee, ahhh." But she knows she shouldn't be touching it because she won't let Shona any closer.

Klara darts round the end of the bed and Shona saunters behind while Klara's shouting, "Baybee!" at the earplug. Shona doesn't care about the earplug, just the fact it's already been used. Klara's touching Shona's ear gunk. And it's small enough to choke on. And that would be all she needed. Shona wouldn't have a clue how to call a Spanish ambulance. The language barrier catches her tongue – is there any point in saying the word earplug? She'll only have to explain, *I put them in so I can't hear your dad's pre-bed shower, but they fall out during the night so I wake to the sound of chair legs and cisterns.*

Who's she kidding? She does care. *That's my earplug give it back!* she wants to insist, like a three-year-old. Anyone at all could rent the other bedroom and good sleep is the one thing making the trip bearable. Why is she regretting not childproofing her room when she shouldn't have had to childproof her holiday let?

The girl has done another circuit around the bed and is kneeling on it, head turned towards Shona, ready to spring away. *You have my time, you have my attention, but you don't have me dancing like a marionette.* Shona reaches for her toiletry bag on the chair, looks inside and gasps, "Oh wow!!" It's almost cruel how easy this trick is to pull off. She clasps Klara's distracted hand and prises it with stronger fingers. The earplug drops and Shona grabs it. Klara begins whimpering. Shona lifts her washbag and walks to the bathroom knowing Klara will follow because she won't like solitude for any length. Leaving the room is the tactic Shona should have employed minutes earlier.

Klara presents her brushed teeth for inspection. She doesn't get the chance to argue about getting into bed because Shona keeps her occupied with talk of bedtime stories. "Will you read to me, Klara? I liked the story you read before." Shona has lifted Klara level with the bookshelf. "You can choose," she says.

"Thees book." Klara rushes to the bed and arranges herself under the covers. She pats her hand where Shona should sit. Klara appears to channel a school marm while telling Shona a very short Danish story sprinkled with the English words 'cat', 'today' and 'no no no!'

Shona's struck by the complete trust of this girl. Shona

can't fall asleep if her neighbours bring friends back after the pub, and here's this child beside someone she barely knows, presuming everything's good, presuming the stranger is looking out for her as she nods off. *Quite right for testing me, wee one; for showing that you're no pushover. What means have you, other than a bit of rebellion, a bit of resistance*?

Shona waits till she's sure Klara's asleep. She turns off the lamp and nips downstairs to put lights off and collect her book. She can stay within earshot if she reads in the spare bedroom. Later, putting the book down, going back to join Klara seems wrong. Why would Shona take herself into a bed with a child she isn't related to? It reminds her of media reports involving washed-up entertainers and dodgy alibis. There's just no need when there are other options. Shona treads gently to collect her phone. She's been keeping it on flight mode and using it like a watch, but marooned in this empty room, she can't resist. She waits a few seconds to let the signal settle. No messages.

Everything is heavy and black when wailing rouses Shona. It takes a second to compute that it's Klara and that Shona's in an unfamiliar bed. She crosses the landing. "Dónde está Mamá?" Klara is sobbing. *Good question. Where* is *your mum?* Shona keeps her voice soft, "Auntie Shona's here." She sits on the duvet and strokes her hand over Klara's hair. "Lucky you, big girl in the big bed. I'm sleeping very close. I'm in the bedroom beside yours."

Klara is a little woodland creature with both thumbs resting on her chin and her scrunched forefingers stroking in circles either side of her mouth. Shona has to control her own breathing; deep, long, silent, deep, long, silent, to circumvent buckling at this girl's tricks learned to soothe herself.

. . .

It's dark when she hears the shutters shunt over the slab and the door-glass rattle. He unlocks his room and opens a drawer. Always barefoot in the house, it's like he's levitated when a cup lands on the kitchen countertop. Then his voice is nearby and before long, the basin taps, the flushing loo. A lie-in isn't going to happen. Shona enters the bathroom when they're done and turns on the shower.

When she unlocks the door, holding her towel in front of her, he's waiting halfway up the stairs, obscured by the balusters. "Hey, everything okay last night?" Literally stripped of any privacy in this house, she replies, "Fine, yeah." He has no right to details. He hadn't sent so much as one text. He isn't moving so she walks to her room feeling no panic to cover herself. Sod him.

Dressed, Shona arrives downstairs to see him clad in tight white underwear, executing press-ups in the passage between the couch and the wall. What a had-a-shag-last-night cliché. Unless this show is for her. *Ugh.* She edges around him. Klara is eating chocolate spread from a jar at the table. Shona fetches an apple from the kitchen and sits near Klara. In anticipation of what will happen next, Shona goes back for a knife and a plate. She cuts the apple into slices at the table, offers Klara one. "Nice hair," she tells her, noticing two neat bunches – the first time she's seen her before nursery. Klara pushes a hair bobble across the table towards her. Shona pulls her own hair into a ghastly contortion, then secures the band around it. "Like this?" she asks. Each time she changes the style it sends Klara wild with giggles.

"Hey," says her dad. He fires Danish instructions, staccato, the same as in any household: shoes, water bottle, quick, Klara, now. "Here." He picks up her sandals, deposits them at her feet and goes to the bedroom, re-emerging dressed and wearing a child's backpack.

When they've gone Shona finishes her apple standing at the threshold. The weather has its familiar dry-for-now quality. She fetches her daypack and stuffs her jacket into the bag.

A while into her stride, a flash invades her earphone reverie and she halts in case it's a car passing but it's a high-speed road bike, powered by a guy in fluorescent apparel. She turns to see a staggered pack of riders and leans her lumbar bone against the wall to let them pass. Big boys' holiday. *Do they come to a halt at every junction, or do they fly on through and let it be the farmer's job to slam on the breaks?* She thinks that's what she would do today. Leave it to fate. Either it would work out, or she'd be mangled to bits. Which she already sort of has been. Although, someone dancing and singing on a purposeless stroll on a Mediterranean island probably doesn't qualify as mangled. Maybe this domestic stint, slowing down and sleeping a lot, is doing her some good. Somebody somewhere is having a worse time of it.

At the door, she notices that the trainers she's kept clean all summer have terracotta clay stains around the toes and soles. *It'll be a fond reminder...* she laughs, kicking them off. Her host is picking up a plastic pouch from the kitchen counter, parting the top with his fingers and inhaling. He does this enough times that it's clear he wants her to notice. She uses it as an opportunity to improve her Spanish. "How do you say in Spanish, 'what are you doing?'"

"Qué haces," he prompts.

"Qué haces?" she asks.

"It's maca," he says. "You know maca?"

Yes, she knows that trendy super-food and how much it costs. "I thought you *ate* it, not sniffed it."

"I feel it in my brain," he answers. "I'm like waaaah!" And he wobbles away, jiggling his arms like he's having a seizure.

Shona is lazy with her lunch dishes. *Fuck it*, is her precise thought. It's mid-afternoon before she makes a move to wash them. The double carton of juice she'd bought is tethered with a gold ring of paper which Shona slides off. Noticing its potential she goes to the courtyard where Klara is playing. She places it on Klara's head with a trumpet fanfare. "The queen!"

Klara grabs it from her head to look more closely. "La corona," she gasps, and places it back on, askew. She looks in the glass of the front door. "La princessa!"

"Síií," says Shona, extending the vowel the way Spaniards do. She sits on the stoop. "Qué haces?" she asks.

Klara has a pail of coloured chalks nearby and she goes to select one, bringing it to Shona. "Blue, lovely, thank you." Klara's holding a pink chalk and she sits back on her heels and starts drawing on a paving stone. "A crown?" asks Shona. "La corona?"

Klara adjusts the marks, adding a jagged line, and says, "Sí. La corona." She moves quickly to the next slab, swapping the pink chalk for a green and producing another crown, whispering each syllable, "La corona."

She looks towards Shona, who returns a thumbs-up signal. Klara taps Shona's chalk to the ground so Shona draws a crown, with a smiling face underneath it and long hair. "The princess, Klara."

Klara gets busy again and when she leans back, she's written her own name, with the 'r' back to front. "Fantástico!" says Shona. "You are one smart girl. You can write? Wow!"

Shona starts to use her chalk and Klara says, "No!", taking it away and giving her the yellow one instead, saying, "Okay." Shona makes a rectangle, divided into eight squares and asks Klara, "What's this?" Klara looks at the drawing and smiles but doesn't know, so Shona erases the corner and redraws it as a bite mark. "Chocolate!" says Klara, and starts copying the drawing.

Shona has noticed it becoming duller around them but hasn't thought more about it, until a millisecond of white sears the air, followed quickly by telltale rumbling. Klara shrieks and Shona is herding her inside and closing the front door. "No!" Klara is objecting. "Chocolate!"

Shona tells her, "We have to come inside when there's lightning." She kneels beside Klara at the door pane to watch it, but Klara's taking the chalk tip and making contact with the tiles. "Klara," Shona says, "not on the floor." Klara doesn't stop though, and doesn't notice the shimmer of light, only ceases her drawing when the corresponding sound breaks in the sky. She's rapt. "What *ees*?"

"Thunder," Shona tells her.

Klara's expression is suspended, stunned. The music from his room stops. There's an exhale of frustration. A power cut. He comes out, saying, "Lot of rain, hey?" and he leans over them to check the front doors are latched, drawing Shona's attention to the water pooling below the frame. She moves Klara back from the puddle and he throws down a towel he must have grabbed from his room. He darts around the perimeter of the downstairs, securing windows and spitting expletives.

Each time thunder booms Klara responds with her entire posture and turns to Shona, amazed, as if something this immense can't be happening.

Shona is straining to keep her emotions under control observing Klara. *Please God fearlessness like Klara's is rewarded; the prize being the good life she will make for herself.* Life will do what it does but learning when to push back, and ways to soothe, can stop the storms from doing too much damage. No one's absence has severed Klara's connection to her own spirit. Shona, too, has a responsibility to rejoin herself, even if someone she loved didn't want to come along on the journey.

She links an arm into Klara's, which flaps around when the heavens rumble. It's possible that this small girl's nature means she's going to be alright. And perhaps he's doing his best. And maybe that'll turn out to be enough.

A yell carries from upstairs which Shona connects to his discovery of her bedroom window and the water which will be pummelling through. She's aware of him running around frantic for rags and a mop, while she stays crouched at the double doors with Klara, watching fat bullets of weighty rain wash away their pictures.

ACKNOWLEDGEMENTS AND CREDITS

'It's A Man I Need' – first published in *Throwaway Lines*, 2012, and *The Glad Rag*, 2013.

'Kissing Lying Down' – first published in *Broadkill Review*, early 2019.

'Tied Up With String' – first published in *The Brooklyn Review*, spring 2019.

'Adm One' – first published in *The Texas Review*, summer 2019.

'And Maybe It Will Turn Out That Was Enough' – first published in *All The Way Home* (Taproot, 2022).

Thanks to Erin Hoover (erinhooverpoet.com) for the phrase 'kissing lying down' during a table conversation in Wings bar, Johnson, Vermont. Thanks also to Sam Boyce (SamBoyce.net) for editorial wisdom, to Claire Wingfield (clairewingfield.co.uk) for publishing skills, and to 1930s designers and D. Reilly for visual inspiration.

ABOUT THE AUTHOR

Kate Tough is a fiction writer, poet and visual poet.

Her novel, *Keep Walking, Rhona Beech* (Abacus, 2019) is available in paperback and audio. It's the second edition of *Head for the Edge, Keep Walking* (Cargo, 2014). The book is a funny and moving account of how a thirty-something office worker in Glasgow, with a clumsy tendency to speak her mind, puts her life back together after it spectacularly falls apart. Readers have noted that the novel reminds them of a book about someone called Eleanor Oliphant, however Ms. Beech debuted prior to that and was fortunate to catch attention at book festivals, in print media and on television. Kate's poetry pamphlet, *tilt-shift*, was Runner Up in the Callum Macdonald Memorial Award, 2017 and her piece, 'People Made Glasgow', was selected as a Best Scottish Poem

2016. Her work was included in *Makar/Unmakar: Twelve Contemporary Poets in Scotland* (2019) and she was an invited poet at STANZA, 2021.

Away from writing, cats who need a helping hand seem to find their way to Kate's back door and they're always welcome.

On a general basis, if she can maintain her phone on silent mode and also swim a few lengths, it's a pretty nice day.

For occasional updates about new work, writing tips and audio clips, subscribe via the button on Kate's website at www.katetough.com.

If you've enjoyed reading this collection, please take time to add a short review on Amazon, Goodreads or any other suitable forum. These are hugely helpful to authors. Thanks.

ALSO BY KATE TOUGH

Keep Walking, Rhona Beech

A laugh (and cry) aloud journey about rebuilding life after everything falls apart.

"Taut and unflinching. Should appeal to fans of TV series Fleabag."
The Lady Magazine

tilt-shift

A pamphlet of found and experimental poetry which was Runner Up in the Callum Macdonald Memorial Award and listed in the *Times Literary Supplement*'s notable pamphlets, 2017.

"Tough's first full-length collection, when it comes, will be one to watch out for." ***The Scotsman***

makar/unmakar

Kate's work is included in this bold anthology showcasing a dozen of the most vital poets in Scotland working outside the mainstream.

"Kate Tough's found poem about barbed wire sizzles with outrage and humour." ***The Herald***

www.ingramcontent.com/pod-product-compliance
Ingram Content Group UK Ltd.
Pitfield, Milton Keynes, MK11 3LW, UK
UKHW041953190726
13854UKWH00005B/1933

9 781838 421908